rry, Bertice.

Jim and Louella's
homemade heartfix
remedy.

8/02

$22.95

33947000956808

| DATE | | | |
|---|---|---|---|
| | | | |
| | | | |
| | | | |
| | | | |
| | | | |
| | | | |
| | | | |
| | | | |
| | | | |
| | | | |
| | | | |
| | | | |
| | | | |
| | | | |

D1283920

# Jim and Louella's

## Homemade Heart-Fix Remedy

ALSO BY BERTICE BERRY

I'm On My Way But Your Foot Is on My Head;
A Black Woman's Story of Getting Over
Life's Hurdles

Sckraight from the Ghetto:
You Know You're Ghetto If...

You Still Ghetto:
You Know You're Still Ghetto If...

Redemption Song

The Haunting of Hip Hop

DOUBLEDAY

*New York London*

*Toronto Sydney*

*Auckland*

# Jim and Louella's
## Homemade Heart-Fix Remedy

A NOVEL

## Bertice Berry

PUBLISHED BY DOUBLEDAY
a division of Random House, Inc.
1540 Broadway, New York, New York 10036

DOUBLEDAY and the portrayal of an anchor with a dolphin
are trademarks of Doubleday, a division of Random House, Inc.

This novel is a work of fiction. Any references to real events, businesses,
organizations, and locales are intended only to give the fiction a sense
of reality and authenticity. Any resemblance to actual persons,
living or dead, is entirely coincidental and certainly not from any real
experiences by the author.

*Book design by Dana Leigh Treglia*

Library of Congress Cataloging-in-Publication Data

Berry, Bertice.
Jim and Louella's homemade heart-fix remedy: a novel/Bertice Berry.
p. cm.
1. Married people—Fiction. 2. Middle aged people—Fiction.
3. Southern States—Fiction. I. Title.

PS3552.E7425 J56 2002
813'.54—dc21
2002073322

ISBN 0-385-50377-6

PRINTED IN THE UNITED STATES OF AMERICA

September 2002
First Edition

1   3   5   7   9   10   8   6   4   2

# Jim and Louella's
## Homemade Heart-Fix Remedy

# CHAPTER ONE

# Discovery

"Possibilities are like promises:
they only work if you work them."

*I*t all started when Jim couldn't get it up. I guess I should find another way to say it, but we just country folks, so that's how we put it. That was two months ago, and he been 'fraid to try ever since. Anyway, we'd been married for twenty-six years and have had more than our share of it in the love department. We youngish still, me somewhere at the end of my fifties and Jim starting in his sixties. We got a lot of love left. I told Jim just that, but it didn't help none. In all our years of marriage and the three before, I've never seen him so upset. Jim has lots of pride and he don't like the idea of not being able to do his business, so I stopped trying to talk sense into him and did the next best thing.

Now, I've learned years before not to take stock in none of those women's magazines. Their sex tips usually include food or Saran Wrap, and Jim didn't like nothing too messy. He say the only thing he wants wet is me. Anyway, whenever things were tough with me and Jim, I pray that God will give me strength, make me humble, and show me where I'm wrong. Then, I talk to the ancestors. I talk to them like they still alive too, but I do it in my sleep and they always know the answers. This time I call on the women: my mama, Aunt T, and Grandma Sadie. They a hoot.

Mama say, "Hey, girl, don't say a word. We know just why we here."

"Uh-huh," Aunt T say. "Jim can't do the do."

Grandma Sadie tell her to hush. She say, "Your man weren't too good *no* time." She say it's better to have a man who have it but lose it all the way once, than to have one who never lose it, but only halfway does it the rest of the time.

Now, I laugh. Grandma Sadie tell me that our problem is that Jim and me done got way too comfortable with each other. She notice we hit it every Wednesday and sometimes on Sunday (depending on how good my fried chicken is). Until then, I didn't know about that connection, but I vow to take more time with Sunday dinner from that point on.

Mama say, "Girl, you need to spice things up a bit. Fix your hair and put on a little makeup."

Mama know that I ain't into nothing too fancy, but I remind her anyway. Aunt T say I need to learn some other positions. She say I got the wife and the mother part down pat, but I need to be a bit more whorish in the bedroom.

Grandma Sadie say, "Hush up, good loving ain't in no makeup, and it certainly ain't in no slutty ways. If the man want a whore, he'd pay one."

Grandma Sadie say the loving in the bedroom is in all the things you do before you get there. She also say me and Jim are real good to each other, better than most, but we need to find one another all over again.

I ask her what she mean, and she say, "Girl, when the last time you rubbed that man's behind?" Before I can act shocked or tell her "never," she say, "Uh-huh, that's what I'm talking about. Jim knows what he got, and he thinks he knows how he likes it. What makes a man hot is making his woman hot. He thinks he knows just what to touch and how to touch it. In all the years you've been married and all the time you were sneaking around before, Jim ain't had to figure out too much. He made you happy in bed because he made you happy in life, but girl, there's a lot more you should be doing."

At that point I want to ask what, but I hear Jim getting

up so I do too. I roll over and see Jim lying on his stomach. I can tell that he's feeling badly because it's Wednesday, and in the morning he's usually feeling like he want it. Most times, but not always, he gets it too. Usually, I wait for him to come to me, but this time I go to him. I rub Jim's behind slow and soft at first. I hear him moaning real low.

"Mmm baby, that feels good," he say.

I rub it some more, and he turn over. And I see what I hadn't seen in a long time. Mr. Jim, that's what I call him, is standing at full attention. Jim so excited he can't wait to say hello to Miss Lou. That's what he call me down there, on account of my name is Louella. Jim open my legs quicker than he usually do. He ain't wait to see if I'm ready, but I didn't care, seeing his joy make me too happy to say anything. As soon as Jim try to get in Miss Lou, he loses himself.

"Dammit, God dammit," he say.

"Take your time, baby," I tell him. My man ain't big on cussing, so I know he upset.

I start rubbing his behind some more, but Jim too shamed to try again. He mumble "sorry" and get dressed and go off to the job he had for as long we been married. I pray that he don't lose that too.

After he left, I went back to sleep so I can ask Grandma Sadie what I need to do. They were waiting for me.

"Girl, I told you. You need to be more seductive," Aunt T was saying.

"Hush up, girl," my mama told her. "Can't you see she feels badly enough?"

"Look like to me she ain't feeling nothing at all," Aunt T said, laughing.

"Be quiet, y'all," Grandma Sadie told them. "Baby, listen, and listen good. I'm gonna give you the magic you need, but you got to add the spice to it. Like I said before, you've been doing the same thing the same way for years. You need to get to know every inch of that man's body and what really makes him feel good."

I tell her I thought I did. She say Jim and me don't know what we like. I figure she on the other side, so she got to know more than I do.

She say, "Baby, what I'm gonna tell you take patience and your 'bility to follow through. You got to do just what I tell you. How you do it is up to you, though."

"Tonight," she say, looking me right in the eyes, "you and Jim sit on this bed and talk about everything you think you want to do, or have done to you. It's gonna be hard, but all you can do is talk. Don't touch him no matter how hard he get. Tomorrow night you can touch each other, but you can't touch it. Then, the next night you can touch it, but don't taste. The night after, taste but don't enter. Then, on the last night, get ready to go on in."

That night, Jim came home tired as always. I cooked him his Sunday chicken dinner, and it ain't even Sunday. Jim smile at me real sweet, but say, "Baby, I don't want to try...let's give it some time."

I tell him, "Fine. I don't want to, but I do want to talk."

I take Jim into the bedroom, which I had cleaned real good. I had changed the bed linens and even sprinkled my best perfume on it.

"Sit down, baby. Now, Jim," I say, "for years we've been doing things the same, but we gonna try something new."

Jim start to tell me how tired he is, but I tell him to listen. He ain't really seen me act like that, but I know he like it. I sit him on the bed and undress him real slow. I never did that before either. When I take off his pants, I let my fingers touch him real light, but then I remember what my grandma say so I stop myself. Then I undress. Now, you got to believe me when I say this...I don't re-member the last time I got naked in front of my man with the lights on, so all this is making him crazy. I'm not as fine as I used to be, but I still look pretty good. I sit down slowly on the other side of the bed, and Jim thinks I'm asking for some.

I tell him, "Tonight, baby, we just gonna talk. Tell me what you like, and then I'll tell you. Tomorrow, you get to touch me, but you can't touch me tonight. Friday you can touch and Saturday you can touch it and taste it. Sun-day, after church, if you still want to, I'll let you in."

With that, Mr. Jim came right to attention, and I was so wet I could have slid right off my bed. Just that little bit of talk done got us hot and ready, but I know that I gotta do just what Grandma Sadie say. So I start.

"Jim," I tell him, "I love the way you moan. It's telling me that it's good. I love the way you pull my knees apart, but I wish you would stroke my thighs and play with my breasts more and my nipples. I know they ain't like they used to be, but I still got feelings. I love your kisses too, but I wish..."

This takes me a while to say, but Jim jump up and say, "What, baby? Just tell me."

Finally, I get to it. "I wish you would kiss Miss Lou. I want you to put those big lips of yours right down there. I want you to kiss it and put your tongue on it."

I was shamed to say all that, but Jim say, "Alright baby." He was about to do it right then, but I tell him it gotta wait.

Then, I say, "Jim, I need you to touch me more. I want you to put your hand on my head like you used to, and Jim years ago, you used to smack me on the behind a little. I won't mind if you do that too."

Jim sure enough was grinning now. So was I. Talking about it made me want to climb on top of him and ride him to kingdom come.

"Jim," I say, "it's your turn."

Jim ain't say nothing, but I open my eyes to see his

hand is holding Mr. Jim and giving himself some good love.

"Jim!" I say. "You gotta wait." I declare. I had to call him three times before he came to.

"Oh yeah. Okay. Sorry, babe. Seem like I kind of got lost."

"It's your turn," I say.

Jim say okay and tell me things that make me want to lose my mind. "Baby," he say in his deep voice, "I want you to act like you can't wait to get it."

"I can't," I almost yell.

"Well, sometimes it seems like you just doing your duty."

I don't say nothing 'cause I know I got something to learn.

"I want you to talk back too," he say. "Tell me what you want. Say it right in my ear. I want you to tell me it's good, that it's always good. I want you to put your mouth all over me."

I'm blushing now, but I try not to show it.

"Everywhere, my chest. I got nipples too, and I want your mouth on them. Baby, I want you to put Mr. Jim in your mouth too. I want you to suck him and lick him good. I been scared to ask you for it, but we talking, ain't we?"

Jim stood up and started fondling himself again.

"We gotta wait, baby," I say.

"I know. I just want to show you how I want it. Is that

okay?" Jim ask. He hold Mr. Jim up with one hand and start stroking slowly with the other. "Take your mouth up and down like this, baby," he say. "Start slow and the suck harder and faster. You can touch my balls too."

That make me want to laugh, but something tell me not to. Jim tell me to suck it 'til he say he want to come. Then he want me to stand up and bend over. He say he loves taking me from behind, but he don't do it too often because it seem like I don't like it. Now I know my grandma was right because I only remember Jim doing it twice, and both times it was so good I commence to crying. Jim must've thought I was sad, and I was too old-fashioned to tell him otherwise. I'm thinking all of this and look over to find Jim done come all over himself.

"Jim, we s'posed to wait," I say. Jim kiss me like he ain't never kiss me before and went to sleep right there in my arms.

The next day Jim wake up singing, and so do I. He called me three times from work, something he used to do back when we just got married.

"Can't wait to touch you," he say.

"Me neither," I whisper.

That night, I undress Jim again, but this time I lay him on his stomach. I open up some of one of my grand's baby oil I found in the back of my cupboard and pour it all over his back.

"Mmm, that's nice," he say.

I rub his shoulders and back and down to his waist. I knead his strong back like I'm making bread.

"Yes, woman," he say between strokes.

Then, I pour baby oil on his behind and down between his legs. I rubbed his behind and slip my oily fingers between his cheeks. It must feel good because he snatched my hands and tried to take me right then.

"Not yet," I whisper in his ear.

"Oh, woman, you driving me crazy," he say.

"You don't know the half," I whisper back.

"Who are you, and what have you done with my wife?" he say, laughing.

"Lay down, man, and let me finish my business."

I oil his legs and rub them hard, front and back. I touch everything but Mr. Jim. Jim trying to get me to, but he know we gotta wait.

"Alright, woman," he say, "your turn."

He lay me down and pour oil right in the crack of my behind. He rubbed my behind until I thought I could see Jesus. I moaned, and Jim moaned with me. He rubbed everything but Miss Lou. I gotta tell the truth and shame the devil, Jim rubbed my feet so good, I thought I would die. I didn't know feet could get you so wet. He start at my feet and worked his way back up. When he got to my breasts, he could have asked me to run down the street buck-naked, and I might have done it! He rubbed my breasts in a way that let me know he had done it before, but not with me. I forgave him right when the thought came to me. I know that he wasn't getting this from me, and part of that is my fault. Besides, we been too far not to know how to forgive. Jim must've somehow felt my thoughts because he started to cry. I told him it was okay and held him. We rocked each other 'til we fell asleep, oily and wet.

The next day was my grocery shopping day. I got up and took a long, hot shower, fixed my hair, and put on a little makeup. Dora, who works down at the market say, "Girl, you look like you been getting some on the side." I want to tell her to hush and that she needs salvation, but I just grin. I couldn't help it, but something about what she said make me feel kinda proud. I push my pride back 'cause the Bible say pride comes before a fall and say, "Thank you." That got other folks whispering, and I let them. We live in a small town. I know folks gonna think and say whatever they want anyway.

That night, Jim came in smiling. He brought me a cupcake from the little bakery, and it ain't even my birthday. This our night to touch Mr. Jim and Miss Lou, and neither one of us can wait. Now, I have always had my husband's dinner on the table for him when he gets home. With the exception of the birth of two of our five children and a time when I wasn't really myself, his meal has always been waiting. Back then, I learned a lot about real love, but I'll fill you in on that later. This time though, I meet him on the porch. I give him some cold, tart lemonade and kiss him right on the mouth. Miss Brown from across the street is looking. I don't care, but Jim do.

"We better go in," he say.

"Let her go in if she don't like what she see."

Miss Brown must've heard me 'cause she did go in, but I saw her curtain pull back and her eye peeping through. Jim sit next to me on the porch step.

"I get to touch it tonight, don't I?" he say right up next to my ear.

His hot, sticky breath on my neck make my nipples stand out at attention, and my behind got real hot. Before I could answer, Jim shock me by slipping his hand up under my dress. Now it was already dark so I know Miss Brown couldn't see nothing, but all of this is new to me. I was sure surprised, but I had one for Mr. Jim too. He reach under my dress and find me naked as the day I was born. I didn't have on a stitch of underwear.

"Louella Givens," he say, calling me by my maiden name.

I grin, and Jim commence to laugh like I ain't heard in years. He pull me by the hand and take me in. We didn't make it to the bedroom though. Good thing the children are grown and moved out of town, 'cause otherwise they'd seen more than they ever wanted to know. Jim lay me down right on the living room carpet and pull my dress up over my head. He start to kiss my breasts, and I remind him that he couldn't use his mouth 'til the next day. He shook his head but said he wasn't going to argue. He grab my breast with one hand and start playing with my nipple with the other. It feel too good to be true. I didn't know my nipple had that much life left in it. Then, I take one of his hands and put it down on Miss Lou.

"You full of all kinds of surprises, ain't you, woman?" Jim say.

He rub across my thighs real light for what seemed like hours. I want to scream, "Touch it, man," but I was learning the importance of patience. By the time Jim stroke the hairs on Miss Lou, I want to skip over the next few days and get right to it. Jim stroked the inside and whispered in my ear, "I love this pussy. This my pussy."

My husband had never talked like this to me before. Three days before I would have been shamed to hear this kind of talk coming from him, but that night I couldn't get enough. He stroked the inside of my kitty until it was hard as him. I was moaning and hollering like I was crazy. Then, when Jim stroked my spot, which by the way I wasn't aware of before then, I squirted all over the place like a man. I was shaking so hard, Jim came right through his pants.

"Woman," he say, "what have we been missing?"

I was panting hard and smiling like a mad woman.

Jim carried me to bed. I felt too weak to touch anything he had, but it was okay. I slept until twelve midnight exactly and awoke to find Jim sleeping like a baby. I waited until one minute past and pulled Mr. Jim out of the slit of his pj's and commenced to sucking him the way Jim showed me. Jim must've done thought he was dreaming 'cause he was moaning something 'bout "No, I'm married. Please don't."

He opened his eyes and saw my mouth on him. I was looking right in his eyes. His head rolled back, and he let out a moan that probably made Miss Brown across the street come to attention.

"I'm coming, baby." When he said that, I climbed on top of him and rocked slowly, allowing him to come inside me. Jim arched his back and yelled, "Sweet Lord, thank you."

"Yes," I say. "I'm coming with you."

We must've both passed out 'cause when I came to, Jim was lying next to me, grinning in his sleep. He woke up and smiled and started kissing me all over. He kissed as high as possible, and as low as possible, then he kissed possible. I stood up and bent over, and we did what we both like. We made love all day long. I fell asleep in between lovemaking, and I saw my ancestors.

"Girl, you was supposed to wait," Aunt T said. "You never did know how to wait."

My grandma smiled. "Girl, hush, sometimes rules are

made to be broken. Besides," she added, "y'all been waiting over twenty years to get it right."

"Thank you," I told them.

Jim must've thought I was talking to him 'cause I heard him say, "You wait, you ain't had nothing to thank me for yet. Come here, woman. Let me taste you."

CHAPTER TWO

# The Cost of Love

After me and Jim learned them sweet love secrets, seemed like life turned upside down. Don't get me wrong, me and Jim felt like we were twenty again. All he had to do was look at me, and things got hot and wet. Jim took to coming home at lunchtime again, and it wasn't for lunch. Things between us was just fine. I just wish I could say the same about the folks in our little town. Ain't no place to start but the beginning. So let me just go on and tell you what happened after me and Jim got our stuff set straight.

The very day after we followed my grandmother's advice, me and Jim had the ability to do more than make love all night. Now, believe me when I tell you, that's powerful enough. We ain't young no more, so going at it for hours was sure something special. Took me a while to walk straight. Anyway, what happened to us was like something out of a movie. Jim went to work, though he didn't want to, just like he always did. I got up early to make his coffee and breakfast, like I always did too.

Well, truth shame the devil, there was a time when I didn't make his breakfast. I told you before that I wasn't always myself. Now, I got to get off the path to show you the way, so let me move back a bit so you get the whole picture. Believe me when I tell you I have always tried to do right by my man, but there have been times when I've been a bigger fool than I care to admit. Jim loves my cooking, always has, but there's something about my breakfast and especially my coffee early in the morning, five in the morning to be exact, that makes Jim smile at me like he been locked away and I'm the first women he see. Anyway, years ago when me and Jim first got married, long before our kids were even a gleam in Jim's eye, I got to feeling kinda low about myself. Jim was sweet as always, but I had been laid off the job that I had at the paper bag factory and couldn't find no work. Jim said that I shouldn't worry since he made enough for the two of us. Anyway, he was hoping that I would stay home and start making some babies. Now, I made him breakfast every day from the first day we were married. But when I got laid off, I didn't have to get up early no more. Still, I got up to make Jim's breakfast just like before. After he left for work, I'd go back to bed for a few hours 'til it made sense to wake up. It was then that I met my neighbor, Lucy.

Now, Lucy means well, but she watches way too much television. To make matters worse, Lucy act like them soap operas and talk shows are all the Bible she need. I ain't into no soaps. Ever since Luke raped Laura on *General Hospital*, and they got married, I have not wanted to see no more of that madness. Imagine if your girlfriend got raped and then married her rapist. You would not go to the wedding unless you were coming with a straitjacket for her and a gun for him. Anyway, when I got laid off, I found that I had neighbors I didn't know. Lucy and her upstairs neighbor, Mae, took to visiting me every morning and sitting there 'til I put them out, which was usually just in time to get Jim's dinner cooked.

"Girl, you running 'round cooking for that man like you a slave or something," Lucy told me one day.

Now, I had already heard from other women that I was too good to Jim. Like you could ever be too good to somebody who was good to you.

"You don't ever do nothing for yourself," Lucy say.

"It's always, 'Jim like this,' or 'Jim don't like that.' You don't have no opinion of your own," Mae say, like

Lucy ain't say it first. "If Jim didn't tell you what he thinks about something, seem like you don't have no thinking on it either."

"Yeah," Lucy say. "When's the last time you went to a movie or restaurant with your girlfriends or alone?"

I wanted to tell them silly women that I have only been to the movies with Jim because we have to go to the one over in Savannah. The theater in our little town didn't allow Black folks in it until ten years after everybody else did. If they didn't want me then, they won't get my money now. On top of that, there ain't been no movie made that's so good that I would drive all the way to Savannah by myself just to see it. Last time we were there, we saw *Waiting to Exhale*. I was in that movie theater wishing all them beautiful Black women would just go on and breathe. Anyway, I didn't say any of this to Lucy and Mae. I just sat silent while they ate my homemade biscuits and drank the rest of Jim's coffee.

"This coffee is cold," Mae say like she was used to something. "Would you please brew some fresh, Louella?" She say it more like a command than a request.

I get up and make it 'cause I was trying to be a good neighbor, but in the back of my mind, I'm deciding that this good neighbor is about to move. That's when Lucy got all up in my business.

"Jim leaves early, don't he, Louella?" she ask.

"Now, I done already tell you that Jim been working

the same job since he was in high school. Everybody in our town know that he work the morning shift, always has, always will. That's how Jim made supervisor by the age of twenty-six. Youngest supervisor ever in that plant. He say he like to go early so he can set his mood straight before everybody else gets there. That way, Jim say he can be at his best for the rest of the day."

"Yeah, he goes early," Mae piped in. "I saw that fine man of yours yesterday when I was coming in from my, uh-um, date." Mae giggled, and Lucy winked at her. They didn't even bother to let me in on their little joke. I didn't say nothin'. My mother always say, "When folks act like they got something that's too good to share, you should let them keep it."

Anyway, Mae ask me what time I have to get up to make the coffee that's now too cold for her. I tell her, and she say I'm crazy.

"If my man had to go to work early, and I didn't, wouldn't be no reason for me to get up early to do no cooking. Well, no kitchen cooking," she say, winking at Lucy. Mae laughed out loud and winked at Lucy again, like I was too dumb to know what she was talking about.

Well, they laughed and talked and winked so much 'til I got to believing some of what they said. Jim did leave early, and I had to be up earlier than he did if I was gonna make his coffee. I didn't know it then, but losing my job had me feeling a little left out of the town's life, if you know what I mean. I wasn't in on all the cafeteria talk or the daily going-ons you find out about from just walking down the street. Now, it's a true shame that sometimes when a person feels left out, they can start to feel bad about themselves, 'cause when you feel bad about yourself, you gonna try to make others feel bad too. That's where I was. I didn't feel a need to dress up too much or even fix my hair since I didn't have no place to go but to church on Sunday. Lucy and Mae had become my eyes and ears for what was going on in town. True, Jim filled me in on most things, but Jim was not one for gossip. Never has been, never will be. He'd share news about somebody being a grandfather or how some young lineman was leaving work because they got a scholarship to college. Lucy and Mae, on the other hand, always knew whose shoes had been found under the wrong bed, or what local girl was leaving town to visit family for the next nine months.

I'm ashamed to tell you this, but I found myself caught up in Mae and Lucy's world. It made me somehow feel important, like I was on the inside of a select group or something. One thing led to the next, and I was sitting around laughing with them two like I didn't have a lick of sense. Then one day, what seemed like out of the blue, I decided I was not going to get up to make breakfast. Now, you know that was hard to do because I had been doing it every day for the two years we had been married. I didn't even need no alarm clock to wake me up. God woke me at four-thirty A.M. every day. Well, this day, I lay there trying to act like I'm sleep. Jim didn't even bother me. He just look at me to make sure I'm okay, then he kiss me lightly on the forehead and went on to work.

When he got home that day, expecting to have dinner, I tell him I'm tired and would like to go out to eat once in a while. I went on to ask him when the last time was that he even thought about buying me flowers or candy. Now, Jim never did talk a lot, and what I was saying didn't make him no more talkative.

"Alright, Louella Johnson," he say.

Later on, I find out that Jim had been thinking on it all day. When I didn't wake up, he figured that maybe I had finally got pregnant and was wanting to go out to surprise him with the news. Jim sat there smiling at me like he was crazy.

"Well, woman, what you trying to tell me?" Jim ask on the way home.

I didn't know what he was thinking, and I tell him so.

"We gonna have a baby, or what?"

I laughed and ask, "Why you think that?"

Jim got silent and mad at me for the first time in our marriage. He didn't say anything else all night. This made me even more determined to take care of myself first, as Mae and Lucy had said I should do. The rest of the week I stayed in bed right up to when my friends show up. We watched TV all day. And I get around to cooking dinner for Jim, but only when I felt like it, usually after he got home. Well, Jim finally asked me if he did something to me and if I was alright. I told him I was fine and getting better. Jim didn't say anything else. He just went to bed on our couch. Now, if you want to hurt me, just take away my peace. Sleeping with Jim I be thinking, "Books was always like fishing. Even if you don't catch nothing, you have a good time." When Jim went down to our couch, I had the nerve to get mad at him. I went to sleep mad, something my grandmother always preached against.

"Don't ever let the sun go down on your wrath," she quoted. "The good book knows what it's talking about," she said.

"Books don't talk," I would mumble.

And she would just say, "Yes they do, and you'd better listen."

That night I guess my anger was enough for my grandmother to visit me in my sleep. That was the first time. I found out later that I was the one who called her. At first, I thought she just came on her own.

"Hey, gal," she say, smiling. "I see you done let a bald woman sell you hair-growing grease."

My grandmother always had a way with words, but in my sleep she was downright clever.

"What you mean?" I ask.

"Girl, you know what I mean. This is your dream," she say. "Lucy and Mae ain't got no man, but you gonna let them tell you what to do with yours."

I immediately got her point, but that don't change me right away.

"Grandma, you know how hard Black women work."

"Yes, I do," she say. "I also know how hard Jim work. Man work like a mule," she added.

"Well, I'm tired of being the mule's jackass. He don't bring me no flowers. He don't take me no place. The man hardly have anything to say outside of what's going on at work. Grandma, he don't even tell me I'm pretty no more."

My grandmother look at me like she was gonna slap me.

Then she say, "I need to ask God how people can start out smart and then turn real dumb. Girl, don't Jim work hard and get a good check?" She didn't stop to let me answer. "Don't he bring that check home to you to do with it as you see fit? Seemed like to me if you needed flowers, you could go and buy them. Don't that man love you like pig love slop?"

I wish she'd used some other comparison, but I know what she mean all the same.

"He reads the Bible to you every night and make love to you so good that your whole body feel new, don't he?"

I was a bit embarrassed to hear my grandmother talk like this, but just as she had said, it was my dream.

"So he ain't sophisticated. He don't do stuff that folks do in soap operas, but that stuff ain't real. Them people sleep in false lashes and sparkly gowns. He does what's true and what truly matters. It don't cost you much, just a cup of coffee and some biscuits."

Well, my mama ain't raise no fool. I woke up and bless my soul, it was exactly four-thirty A.M. I went to that kitchen, fired up my percolator, and rolled the fluffiest biscuits Jim would ever taste. When Jim got up, which was as soon as he smelled coffee, he come stumbling into our little kitchen.

"You sleep okay, baby?" I ask, all cheery.

"Not too good," he mumbled. "But I'm better now," he say, smiling.

Jim ate, and I think I heard him humming. He rubbed my behind and kissed me on the forehead like he always did. "See you later, baby" was all he say, but that was all I need to hear. I was getting my peace back.

Later that morning when Mae and Lucy came over, I met them at the door.

"Can't talk today y'all," I tell them. "I got work to do."

Mae was sniffing at my door. "I smell biscuits. Look like the old Louella is back."

"She sure is," I said, laughing, and I for one am glad. "Now would you all excuse me? I gotta take some time out for me."

I shut the door and got to cleaning that house like you do when you first move into a place. You know how when something is new, you treat it real good, like it's the best thing in the world? After a while though, you start getting tired of looking at the same old thing, and suddenly, you don't give it the attention you use to. I had been treating Jim like an old house that I was tired of living in. Well, I went to fixing that house like it was brand new. Then, I cooked like a woman on a mission, 'cause I was. I was on a mission to do right by Jim. Now, some folks would say that I wasn't liberated, but I'll tell you true, that was the moment that I got my freedom papers. While I was cleaning and cooking up a storm, I saw that real liberation was not in doing what I thought I wanted, or worse still, what somebody else told me I wanted. Real freedom was in me doing what I needed for me and mine.

Everything ain't right for everybody. In other words, my freedom may not look like yours. Take my middle girl, Otha. She's a businesswoman. Don't ask me what kind of business, 'cause I don't know. It's important, though, I know that much. Her husband works in a school where he teaches art. He usually gets home earlier than my Otha, so he does all the cooking. It's a good thing too, 'cause Otha, bless her heart, can't cook a lick.

It wasn't like I ain't try to teach her either. She just wasn't interested. Freedom for her is doing what she was made for. Her husband, my son-in-love, Larry, feels free teaching, painting, and cooking. Cooking for Larry is as natural as cooking is for me. Everybody gotta do what works for them.

Well, I don't need to tell you what happened when Jim got home. He took one look at that place and smelled all them good things coming from the kitchen. You know we got down to business. It was slow and careful like. Jim moved up inside of me like he was afraid of breaking me. And I guess he was. He wanted to make sure stuff stayed like it was. Chile, I did too. After we make love, as y'all call it—back then we called it "doing the do,"—Jim scratched my scalp so good that we went right back to it. This time it wasn't slow and careful. It was fast and strong like we were hungry for each other. When I woke up from my love sleep, I saw Jim staring at me and eating a plate of food that I had made earlier.

"This sure is good, huh, baby?" he ask like I was eating too.

"Sure is," I say, 'cause I know he wasn't just talking 'bout that food.

He was talking 'bout us, 'bout our life and how we had decided to live it. I knew for sure right then that my grandmother was right when she say Jim love me like a pig love slop. It ain't the prettiest picture you want to conjure up when you thinking 'bout love, but it fits. It's natural like rain. Sometimes it'll mess up your hair, but it makes all the right stuff moist enough to grow right.

Well, I told you all of that to tell you 'bout how things in our little town changed after we learned them sweet love secrets. I guess I got way off on a bend. I do that sometimes, but like my mama used to say, "It'll all come out in the wash."

# CHAPTER THREE

# Change Is Gonna Come

After me and Jim listen to my ancestors and got their love secrets, we got a lot more than we bargained for. I didn't notice it at first. Sometimes change come sudden; sometimes though, it come so easy that it make things seem natural.

I was at the Farmers' Market, which is where you can find me every Tuesday morning. I go over there when the farmers first come in and lay everything out. I love watching them place their produce with all the love and commitment anyone could have in their work. Anyway, that morning I was waiting for things to get started when I hear Mr. Stan, that's the best fruit grower we got 'round here, say, "Seem like that woman just ain't interested no more. Don't know what I did. I'm just trying to love her. Maybe I'll go someplace else, see how she like that."

Now, I'ma tell you true, 'cause there ain't no other way to tell it. I was watching that man and hearing him talk, but I ain't see his lips move. If I'm lying, I'm flying, and you don't hear me tweet. That man's thoughts were just as loud as if he was saying them. I went to looking all over, to see if maybe somebody else was talking, but I know it's him 'cause he got this hurt look on his face that goes right with the words I'm hearing. As I live and breathe, I'm thinking something's wrong 'cause I ain't never had no gift like that. My grandma, and a few of my cousins, can see and hear, but I've always had to live by my wits. Well, I'm listening closer now 'cause something powerful is happening. I learned long ago that when change comes, you gotta slow down and take note of it. In the midst of that change is all the possibility in the world. Well, I got to hearing Mr. Stan complain about how his wife don't like his touch and how she never want to do the do no more. All the while he saying this and touching them fruits like Jim been touching me, real soft and special. I want to yell to Mr. Stan, "If you touch her like you holding that orange, she'll let you do anything you please." But I don't say nothing. Mr. Stan don't know me like that, and he sure don't know that I can hear him thinking. If he could, he would've been more careful with all them thoughts.

I watch Mr. Stan for longer than usual. It occurred to me that maybe I can hear other folks. I walked along the market aisles trying to see if I could. But just like a child who's misbehaving, it don't happen when folks are watching. I tried not to concentrate too hard, and that only made me think harder. I went down to Mr. Blue's stand, 'cause he always been easy to read, even for me. That's 'cause the man tells every and anybody just what's on his mind.

"Morning, Mrs. Johnson. I see you on your regular rounds. Did you hear about Maybelle's youngest girl, Miltonia, the one they call Toni? Well, it seems that Toni ain't just short for Miltonia. That girl don't like men, from the way I hear it. They say she done run off with a white girl from up North. Now, if she was my child, I'd a put her in her place. Girl oughtta know what she was made for. Nuts are made for bolts, not another nut."

I was wishing I could just hit that man with a slab of his own salt pork, but I didn't say nothing. Least I didn't think I did. Out of nowhere, Mr. Blue's face turn funny.

"What you say, gal?" he ask me real hard like.

"I didn't say anything, Mr. Blue," I tell him, wondering if he been eating too much of his own pork. "I was just listening to you talk about Miltonia. She is a nice girl. You have to admit that. The way she took care of her mother when she fell and hurt herself."

Mr. Blue look at me like I broke wind in church during

prayer. "Don't go changing no subject. I heard you loud and clear. You of all people need to stay out of other folks' business."

Now, as I live and breathe, I ain't know nothing 'bout what he was trying to say. That me "of all people" line could have set my mind on edge for the next two years, add to it the fact that Mr. Blue was accusing me of being in people's business. This was a man who believed that all business was his. Well, the Bible say not to argue with a fool, so I ain't say nothing.

"Don't look at me like you don't know what I'm talking about, Louella Givens," he say, calling me by my maiden name.

If I hadn't had the experience I had earlier with Mr. Stan, I'da just thought that ole Blue done finally snapped. You know you can only be in other folks' business for so long before you realize that you done left your own unattended.

"I heard you, girl," Mr. Blue said. "What you know about it anyway?" he asked.

I still didn't say nothing 'cause I ain't know what he was talking about.

"Did my girl tell you? I should've known she would've gone and told somebody. I ain't do nothing to her. I didn't get a chance to," he mumbled.

I stood there, trying to figure the whole meaning of what he was saying when I heard my own voice in my head having a conversation with the voice that must have been coming from ole Blue's head. If I didn't know myself like I do, I'da ran all the way home from that market. Something told me to be still and listen. And usually when folks say that something is talking to them, they mean something bigger than themselves, something they can't fully understand.

Well, the voice in my head say, "The only reason you didn't do anything to your daughter was because your wife walked in. Thank God. But you went around town telling folks you put her out for cheating on you. Say that daughter wasn't yours, but she is, and you were trying to use her, like she was your wife. I'm glad that woman chose her daughter over you. Miltonia's mama wasn't as bright as your wife, so anything that girl becomes you and all the men like you done had a hand in her pain. Now that she chooses joy, how dare you talk dirty about the way she choose to live her life? As you say, you of all people should know better."

Well, as I'm telling you now, I know that God had a hand in this. Blue got to crying like a baby. He grab hold of me. I didn't know what he was gonna do next. But all he did was hold me and cry. In my head I heard him talking 'bout the dirty things his daddy made him do and all my anger turned to pity. Good thing it was early in the morning and there weren't many people around, 'cause anybody watching me holding ole Blue while he crying would have called the doctor for both of us. My mind told his that things had to stop with him, otherwise that cycle of hurt was just gonna keep on going. I let him know that he gotta do right by his daughter and all the children she gonna have and the ones after that.

"What can I do?" his mind ask me.

"You ain't been sending nothing to them, but you know right where they are."

Now, I'ma tell you I was still kinda scared about all this in my head, but at the same time, I was somehow calm. Like it was as natural as a rainbow after a storm. You still stop and look at it in amazement, even though you've seen it before. I had known about special gifts, but I only knew of folks being born with them. I started to figure that something 'bout what happened with me and Jim done caused me to be born into something new.

"Send that woman and your child a letter. Tell them what you told me. All of it. Let them know that your evil didn't start with you. Ask for forgiveness, but don't ask for them to come home. They got a new life over in North Carolina now. Send your daughter money every month. You got plenty. Set some aside for her college. She's a smart girl, and she's gonna make you proud."

"And Mr. Blue," I said this part out loud as much for my own hearing as for his. Incredible things call for credible proof. I wanted to make sure that this was real, and Mr. Blue needed to be sure so he could set himself and his child free. "Stay outta folks' business. Looking for dirt in other people's houses ain't gonna make yours no cleaner." Well, that man thanked me out loud, and I walked on just like a rainbow after the rain. Sure was an amazing thing that happened, but it was natural just the same.

When I knew that I wasn't crazy, I went back by Mr. Stan and his fruit. He was still setting things up. By now he was arranging strawberries into fancy baskets folks buy to impress themselves. I knew that what I was experiencing had come to me for a reason. God don't give you power just for yourself. Wouldn't be no use in having it.

I decided to be a little more careful than I'd been with Mr. Blue.

"Morning, Mr. Stan," I say, trying to act like I had no idea what had been on his mind. "You know why I came down here so early, Mr. Stan?"

He look at me and shake his head no. I know he thinking that he wish I would leave him alone so he can do his work, 'cause I can hear his voice in my head saying so.

"I come early to watch you work. You got the touch, I do declare," I say, acting like I've seen uppity people do. He kind of smile 'cause he done sold fruit to everybody since he was a boy so he know just which ones I'm imitating even better than I do.

"You know what's really special though, Mr. Stan? It's not just the fact that you grow the sweetest, firmest, roundest fruit anybody will ever have," I say, trying to be diplomatic, "but it's that you know how to handle them. You take your time. You touch them like they a young, fresh—ooh Lord, listen to me talk," I say, watching Mr. Stan as he hanging on every word. "If Jim Johnson heard me carrying on like this, he wouldn't even let me eat your fruit."

That made Mr. Stan laugh, and I'm glad 'cause I got his attention in a way as not to shame him with what I'm about to say.

"Don't get me wrong when I tell you this, 'cause ain't no woman can be happier than Mrs. Louella Johnson, but Mr. Stan, if you treat your wife half as good as you treat them fruits, good Lord, man, that woman must be a grateful soul."

Right then and there, Mr. Stan's face fell like a crate of berries off the back of his truck.

"Well, I'll tell you the truth, Mrs. Johnson," he say. "My wife don't seem too happy with me lately."

Woo, I'm so proud of myself I almost pat my own back. I'm so glad that I got him to confide in me that I don't know what to do. He don't have no idea that the thoughts in his head are being heard loud and clear by yours truly, and I had no plan to tell him.

"What's wrong, Mr. Stan?" I ask like I don't already know.

"Well," he paused and looked me over good, "maybe you can help. You a woman."

"Last I checked," I say, trying to keep things as light as they can get when I know this man's heart so heavy.

"My wife, Irma, don't seem like she want me no more." Mr. Stan was looking at the ground like this answer might grow up outta there.

"What you mean she don't want you? Irma Allen loves the ground you plow, Mr. Stan."

"I don't mean she don't want to be married to me. We still like berries on a vine, kind of connected, if you know what I mean. Only having problems..."

Mr. Stan's embarrassment had come back up, causing him to choke on the truth. "I don't want to bother you with none of this, just something telling me you might understand."

There it was again. That something telling me. "Mr. Stan," I say, "how long I been buying fruit from you?"

He blow air through his nose the way grown men do when they letting you know they grown. "I guess 'bout as long as I been selling it."

"I'm glad you remember. We went to school together, boy. My mama bought fruit from your daddy. And I been knowing you as long as we both been Black. Your wife and I don't know each other that well 'cause you had to go get you a city girl and all, since none of us country girls was good enough."

Now, I knew that Mr. Stan didn't feel that way. I was

just trying to poke a little fun and lighten his load. Sometimes when folks laugh, they can see better.

"Louella Givens, you know you never gave me the time of day. You was the one that was too good for anybody but that Jim Johnson. You locked eyes on him and went blind to the world around you."

"Gone and tell the truth, Stanuel Allen." Now we both laugh, so I know he ready to deal with his heart.

"Well, Mrs. Louella, seem like I don't turn my baby on no more like I used to. I know I done gained some weight and my belly get in the way of our business. I done lost most of my hair too. But Irma ain't as young as she used to be either. Still, that don't matter to me. I see the same woman I married going on twenty-five years ago."

Mr. Stan turned sad again, and I could now feel his heart. This gift was quickly becoming a burden. I took Mr. Stan's hand. It was rough and callused from all the farmwork he did. When he held my hand, I found it hard to believe that these were the same hands that had so lovingly touched them berries just a short while before.

"Mr. Stan," I say, getting right to the point, "did Irma ever tell you that you a little rough?"

He looked at me through slit eyes and ask, "Why? She tell you something?"

I wanted to tell him that his city wife didn't have much use for any of us country folks, but I know that was just my feelings getting in the way and that this conversation was not about me.

"No, she ain't tell me that, but like you said before, I am a woman. And well, sometimes for women we say one thing, but we mean something else. Now, I love my man and my boy children, but sometimes they can be dumb as rocks. If women could see the power they have over men, they would never sit up crying about not having one. No sirreebob, They would use they power to get whatever man they wanted."

Mr. Stan must have believed me when I said if we say one thing, it has a meaning all women understand, 'cause he went on and told me everything. He talked 'bout how he worked so hard to buy all the pretty things his wife loves. How he try to make sure she's happy 'cause he still, to this day, can't believe she married him. Her daddy ran a clothing store and his daddy was just a farmer. It took all the Jesus in me to keep from saying, "Fool, your daddy own his own land. Her daddy just worked for somebody else." I don't know what it is that makes my people think that dressed-up slavery is freedom. Anyway, I let him talk. He tell me 'bout how hard it was for her daddy to accept him. How he worked to show them uppity Negroes, my words not his, that he would treat that girl right. Now, for what it's worth, Irma wasn't no fool. She knew a good thing when she saw one. She fell in love with Mr. Stan when she first laid eyes on him. Who wouldn't? The man was always easy to look at. But there are some folks who wear their goodness right on they face. Mr. Stan was one of them. He got them smiling eyes, that tear up at anything sensitive. He just a good ole soul, and anybody with any kind of sense can see that.

Mr. Stan went on to tell me how he and Irma wanted to have a bunch of kids, but she couldn't. Even that was okay by him. His mama had a bunch of kids, so all his brothers and sisters had a bunch of kids too. He always had plenty of nieces and nephews to love. Still, I think Irma knew that a man like Mr. Stan need kids to pass his life and spirit on to. I wanted to ask how come they never took in no kids, but I didn't even have to. Mr. Stan tell me on his own. He say that Irma didn't want no one else's children, that it just didn't seem right to her. So they were now smack-dab in the middle of life without children, growing farther and farther apart. I could see Mr. Stan's sadness, and just like with Mr. Blue, I was starting to feel it. I wanted to give him the recipe that my grandmother gave to me and Jim, but something tell me that it was just for us. I somehow knew that the answer to each person's problems had to come from their own pain. My grandmother use to tell us that the way out was back through. I was starting to see the meaning in this.

"Mr. Stan," I ask, "when did the change happen in your life with Mrs. Irma?"

Mr. Stan look down at the ground again and start to thinking. "Hmmm, seem like it was back when I started planting tobacco, 'bout fifteen years ago."

I almost laughed, but I held it in. Mr. Stan's whole life revolve around the rotation of his crops, but he didn't even know it. Now, I have never really been one to do much farming. You may think that everybody who lives in a country town live on a farm, but not me. Sure, there were a few summers when I was young that I worked the harvest for one of my uncles, but I found no joy in it. Always reminded me of slave stories I read when I was young and the stories my great-grandmother use to tell us. I found no reason to pick something I could just go and get from the market. That's the other good thing 'bout living in a little country town that's trying to be citified. We got everything fresh, and even though you might not have grown it, chances are you know who did. Anyway, I get to thinking about what Mr. Stan is telling me, and I ask him what's different about planting tobacco. Well, he go into some long drawn-out explanation about how you have to give it more attention that anything else, then you got to drag it, bag it, and dry it, braid it, and on and on. I'm thinking to myself, *No wonder things changed.* He was spending more time with the tobacco than he was with

Irma. Now, hear me when I tell you this: Life is seasonal, and everything has its own time. Sometimes we miss the perfect moment for something 'cause we busy with something else. My spirit started telling me that Irma may have been ready to adopt or even have kids of her own, but Mr. Stan was busy taking care of his tobacco. I was wondering how anybody could hold on to sadness for fifteen years when I saw that folks don't do it all at once. Sadness and pain can creep in on you like a weed takes over a yard. One day you got beautiful roses. They'll grow as long as it rains. But if you don't tend to them, weeds will choke the beauty right on outta that garden. That's what was happening with Mr. Stan and Mrs. Irma. While he was tending his farm, he had left his life unattended. Now, believe me when I tell you I don't know how I knew what I did, but it came to me quick and clear, just like the truth. You see, pain creeps up on you, but joy and truth come in like a rushing wind. I believe that's why some folks are afraid of changing for the good. It's too different, too sudden. They get used to they pain, and they know how to live with it. Joy comes, and they gotta learn something new.

"Mr. Stan," I say, "you got any of that tobacco on you?"

He say, "Girl, I always carry a bit of my own chew."

He get to grinning 'cause he so proud of everything he grow, and I see the other reason why the love life ain't too sweet. The tops of that man's teeth were dark brown from tobacco stains. He handed me the chew, and then I do something I ain't ever done in my life. I chewed it, just as sure as my name is Louella Johnson. That tobacco taste like life. It was real bitter at first, but the more I chew it, the sweeter it gets. Then I start to see. Everything came to me in one big flash, and it was, as my mama used to say, enough to make a gorilla go bald.

"Mr. Stan," I say real quickly, "what I'm gonna tell you came to me from your own mind and your own emptiness. Please don't think that I'm forward or loose, but I got to talk to you direct."

Mr. Stan looking at me like I'm crazy, but he's desperate too, so I know I got his ear.

"You do exactly what I tell you to do, and don't change nothing. I guarantee you that everything will be just fine."

I took Mr. Stan's hand and prayed with him the prayer I use when things ain't right with me and Jim. "Lord, help my brother here to be strong, and then Lord, show him where he's wrong."

Mr. Stan look me dead in the eyes, and I know he's ready to listen. That's when I prayed that I would tell it right.

# CHAPTER FOUR

# The Thing Between Your Thighs

Mr. Stan and I sat down on two old fruit crates, and I start to tell him the things he never learned.

"Mr. Stan, you done just about drove poor Irma crazy. You too easy, and too rough at the same time. Don't ask me how I know, 'cause I'm not too sure of it myself. You wouldn't sell fruit that's rotten or even dirty, would you?"

Mr. Stan shake his head no.

"Well, you need to clean yourself up better for Irma."

Mr. Stan look kinda embarrassed when I say it, and I see he's about to be defensive. But before he can say a word, I tell him to just listen. I grab an orange and rip it open real rough like. Mr. Stan look like I had hurt him.

I say, "Now, is that the way to open fruit?"

Again, he shake his head no.

"Well, that's what you been doing."

Then he start looking sad. I tell him not to, 'cause hurt feelings can't fix his love life. Then I take the skin off that orange and throw the fruit away. He start to laugh, and I'm glad, 'cause I was afraid he was gonna be raving mad at the way I was treating his precious produce. He laugh real hard and say, "I get your point."

Then I grab another orange, and I peel back the skin real slow, all the while I tell him the things he need to hear.

"A woman is like a ripe piece of fruit. She has to be picked at the right time. She has to be ready. You gotta stroke her from top to bottom before you go inside, 'cause if you go inside before she's ripe, she ain't gonna be juicy and you ain't gonna like the taste. You know better than anyone, Mr. Stan, that plucking fruit before it's ready leads to a bad crop the next year."

I take Mr. Stan's rough hand and guide it all over that orange. I thank God again that I made them rounds early, 'cause I don't want folks to start no gossip on me. Mr. Stan squeeze that orange hard enough for it to bounce back, but soft enough so that it don't break. When he did that, I thought about the way Jim holds my small breasts. Once when I notice him smiling at the way that beautiful actress, Loretta Devine, bounced all over the movie screen, I asked him if he wished my breasts were bigger. He smiled and told me that for him anything more than a mouthful was too much. That made me happy. It also told me that looking and liking don't always lead to leaving. Mr. Stan had closed his eyes and was seeing where he had been wrong. I take the orange from him and hand him a honeydew melon.

"Same thing applies," I say.

He thumped the melon and put his ears to it, allowing the echo inside to tell its ripeness. Right then and there, Mr. Stan sat that honeydew on his lap and started rolling it back and forth real slow. I was thanking my blessed stars that I hadn't given him a watermelon. The whole while he's rolling, I'm talking to him. Telling him about the seasons of love. How sometimes things can look dead and hard, like a ground after harvest, but that don't mean it ain't no good. Any farmer worth spit knows that all you have to do is show that dirt some love, and it will be rich and green in its time. If you leave it unattended though, one season after the next, that ground gonna shrivel up and give you grief. It can come back, but you gotta work it harder than ever, harder than you work the tobacco. I tell Mr. Stan he gonna have to win his wife back like he courting her all over again. He gotta clean up and let her see him the way he was before the tobacco.

"You know you can't plow her right away," I say. "You

gotta soften that soil first. Take that woman out, show her off like you used to. Turn the ground. Let her know that you still think she the best wife a man can have. Then, when you done turning that ground for a while, plant the seed and water it. Do it regular like you used to. Whisper in her ear like you talk to them fruits. Tell her that she gonna grow even prettier 'cause you gonna plant yourself inside her 'til the love come back. Touch her like you touch them fruits, soft and special. When you see that first yield, you don't leave it to tend to something else, do you? Naw, that's the time she gonna need even more attention, and you give it to her, 'cause that ground been left too hard for too long."

That's when he start to cry. Now, this was the second time in this the early morning that I done seen a grown man cry. Both of them had seen the inside of their faults. That was sure heavy stuff for me to deal with, but I know that God don't give us more than we can bear without showing us a way out. I done already told you, the way out is back through.

When Mr. Stan was through crying, I told him to close down his stand. Believe the truth when I tell you that man didn't bat an eye. Even though it was early in the morning, he packed up without one bit of hesitation. Didn't take long neither. He was grinning and humming like a schoolboy after his first kiss.

As I watched him drive away, I began to hear things

again. Other customers had started to come up, so my head was getting pretty crowded with noise. I know it's time for me to leave too. The whole way home I tried to make sense out of what was happening. Instead of getting any reason behind the madness, I just got more madness. When I stopped at the light in front of the lower school crossing, I could hear the volunteer crossing guard thinking 'bout the little boy he was escorting across the street. Then I hear the new school principal wondering if the gym teacher would meet him in the locker room again. I was glad when the light changed so I could get away from other people's business. When I drove the same streets I had been driving for years, it was like I was seeing them for the very first time. The little corner liquor store oozed sorrow out onto the sidewalk, and I was shocked when I felt almost the same thing at the storefront church.

Then I got a hold of something that felt like Jim taking me by the hand. When I stopped the little car that I have owned for going on nine years, I was in front of my own house and hadn't even realized it. I had been going by feelings and not by sight when I came to myself. There sitting on the front step was my Jim with his head in his hands. He looked up as soon as the car stopped and ran over with the same quickness that once saved our oldest boy from being hit by a truck.

"Louella, something's going on," he said, panting.

"I know about it, baby," I say, getting out of the car.

"I think I'm going crazy, Louella, and I can't stop it."

"You gonna be alright," I tell him. Jim's eyes were 'bout the size of half-dollars and filled with tears. I looked down and saw that his hands were shaking too. Now, believe me when I tell you again that women got power they don't even know about. Having a menstrual cycle ain't just about bleeding. It's about the cycle of life. It cleanses and prepares us to deal with birth and death. Too often we focus on the pain without seeing the plan. I know that my being a woman is what kept me from being as crazy as Jim was thinking he was. I took my baby by the hand and led him inside.

"What is this?" he ask, all desperate.

We walked up the same six steps we've always walked, but knew those steps into our house would never be the same. Jim saw the vision the same time I did; folks were coming to our house so we could tell them what they would need. I knew that I was gonna have to do a lot of praying. I just didn't know right then how much.

# CHAPTER FIVE

# Scratching at the Pain

When me and Jim got inside, I tell him 'bout what happened down at the Farmers' Market.

"From the way I see it," I tell him, "It got something to do with what happen with us. It's all that love power we done got."

Jim look at me confused like and say that what he seen ain't have nothing to do with love. He say that folks he been knowing all his life were thinking things he would never have imagined. Mr. Broadnax, who work on the line he supervises, was wondering what it would be like to have his big lips on Jim's business. Now, believe me when I tell you I didn't want to hear no more than I had already been through today. But when I got married,

I told God and all them folks watching that I would be with Jim through sickness and in health. I wasn't quite sure which of the two this thing of ours would fall under, but I knew that Jim needed me as much as he ever would.

"Baby," he say, "on my way home I heard Miss Tredgill's thoughts. She is a lonely, lonely woman." Jim paused like he was trying to find just the right words. "She ain't never had no loving in all her life, and she got to be older than our oldest child."

Now, Jim and I both knew that this was the case, since Miss Tredgill taught our oldest and every child that followed. I felt Jim's sadness for her, as if it were my own.

"Baby, what we gonna do about this?"

His eyes were pleading with me, but I felt the determination in his heart. Jim Johnson has always been a man of action. If he see something wrong, he don't stand around wondering who made it that way. He don't join up with organizations and clubs who spend their evenings talking about what they think might be the best way to fix it. No sirree. My Jim just gets right to the solution.

When the dip in the road by the high school got so big that it was a ditch, Jim went right down to his boss, borrowed the tools and men he needed, and fixed it. Everybody else had been talking about what needed to be done, but Jim just went on and did it. That's what I was hearing him say now. The pain of other people's problems was more than he wanted to bear, but he knew that he would do whatever necessary to fix them. Then I see the power behind our love. He got the drive to get up and do it, and I got the ability to figure out what needs to be done. God sure is good.

"Well," I say out loud, even though we hearing each other without talking, something we are definitely gonna have to get used to, "what you want to do, baby? We can't just hang a sign in our window saying JIM AND LOUELLA'S SEX SOLUTIONS."

Jim get to laughing, and I'm so glad. It's hard to have to see your love bearing burdens.

"No, baby," Jim say. "Who gonna come to us for love solutions? Young folks think we too old, and old folks think we too foolish. Maybe we should just sleep on it," he say, grinning.

Now, when he say "sleep," I know that ain't what he thinking. I would've known it even without the gift of hearing. I knew 'cause he was grinning and taking off his shoes at the same time.

We didn't even bother to go into the bedroom. The things we'd experienced left us hungry for what we had together. Good love that was sometimes slow and tender and sometimes hot and quick. Right now, we needed hot and quick. Jim didn't bother to undress me. He just pull off my panties. He did it fast enough to surprise me, and sure enough to let me know how much he was wanting me. Something 'bout being wanted like that, that make me dizzy and wet. Jim put his head between my knees and start kissing my kitty. Now I'ma tell you true, the first time he did it, I wasn't so sure of myself. Me kissing Mr. Jim seem okay to me 'cause it ain't all wet and messy. Not at first anyway. But I got to thinking that it wasn't sanitary for Jim to be down there like that. As I said, that was the first time. Since then, I have taught myself to enjoy the same thing I was taught not to. Jim get to flicking his tongue back and forth, back and forth real fast. So fast that I think I'm gonna explode. Just when I was about to, he ram Mr. Jim deep inside me. He didn't rock back and forth though. He just hold it there real firm. Well, I screamed and he hollered with me.

"I am your man. You are my woman, and we belong together."

He say this like it's our first time, and I'm feeling like down there it is. Everything was so tight and new that I wanted my mama. Jim held me for a long while, real firm, then after a while, he just kinda melt into my arms. Now, if I had known that taking my grandmother's advice was gonna bring as much pain as it did pleasure, I don't know if I would've listened. But laying there with Jim was making me know that it was gonna be worth whatever we went through.

Before either of us wanted to move, the telephone

rang. Jim answered, 'cause he knew who it was. It was Mr. Broadnax from work, wanting to know if Jim was okay since he never once left work sick. Mr. Broadnax had something else on his mind though, but he wouldn't say it and didn't have to. We could hear loud and clear that Mr. Broadnax, one of the biggest flirts in town, was now trying to flirt with Jim. He hoped that Jim wouldn't know. Part of Broadnax's thrill was in holding the thoughts he had to himself. He lived a lonely life because he would never tell the truth about who he was.

"I'm fine," I heard Jim bark. "And if you want to stay well, you'd better keep your mind off my private parts." Jim hung up the phone with more force than I'd ever seen.

I was wondering about poor Mr. Broadnax when I heard Jim say, "Come here, woman, I need you."

# CHAPTER SIX

# *The Calm Before the Storm*

$\mathcal{M}$e and Jim stayed in our house for three whole days. It was the first time in our lives together that we done anything like that. Jim called in to work and told them he wouldn't be in. They asked if he was alright, and he said he would be. Now, no one ever knew Jim to up and take days off, so they thought that something had to be real wrong. Jim don't take to lying, so when they called back on the second day to ask if me and Jim were okay, he told them we were both fine and getting better. It was sure hard for him to say that, 'cause the phone rang just when I decided that my breakfast that morning would be Mr. Jim. When he hung up the phone, Jim pulled me up to him and just stared at me real serious like. Then, he let out his big, deep laugh and hugged me.

"Woman, what we gonna do with all this loving?"

I lay back down next to Jim to think on what he was asking. We have not always been able to enjoy each other's company in silence. That was one of the things I had to grow into. If you haven't figured it out by now, I am the talker in this family. When I was younger, I use to feel like I had to fill in the silence between us. Both me and Jim are from big families, his mama had nine, and mine, eleven. My family talked all the time. Folks always thought it was an amazing thing. Whenever they came into our house, we'd all talk to them at the same time. Funny thing was, we could hear each and every conversation while we was talking. Anybody who was new to our family always had a hard time trying to get into our conversations. We'd laugh at how company would start to say something, then stop when we would join in. Sometimes people would even raise their hand like they were in school or something.

"Ahem, may I please make my point?" Evangelist Richards yelled one night.

Now, Mama always had the visiting preachers over for dinner when they came through for revival meetings. They talked about her good cooking all up and down the circuit. Most times, the first thing a preacher would say when he got to town was, "I sure do hope I'm gonna get to go over to Deacon and Mother Givens' for dinner. I hear she makes fried chicken so good that it'll make you wanna cry for your mama."

"You'll get there," our pastor would tell them, "but leave room for her strawberry cobbler, 'cause just the smell alone will make you preach better."

The ministers loved Mama's cooking. One of them even loved my sister enough to get her pregnant, but I'll tell you 'bout that later. I was trying to tell you 'bout the way we all talked at the same time. Anyway, we talked so much we were able to cover lots of topics and move on to another. Anyone who had something to add could do it, that way we got the goods on what we were saying real quick and could go on and learn something else. The night that preacher tried to jump into the conversation or make his point as he was saying, we all laughed and started talking again. That's when my sister, Esther, pulled the young evangelist aside to tell him how things worked at our house. Musta been a real heated conversation that night, 'cause none of us, including my mama, who watched us like a hawk, ever noticed the two of them laughing and making plans for the next day. Whatever it was we was talking about got replaced in our minds with what happened later. Esther is older than me by three years, so she was going on twenty-one. That was a little old for some folks back then, and she was still unmarried. Daddy thought it was because she like learning more than she liked any of the men in our town. I thought it was for a different reason. Now, believe me when I tell you that I love my sister Esther, but she always had a way about her that said she thought she was better than somebody else. We all wore handed-down hand-me-downs, and we shared everything we had. That was a rule in our house. You couldn't bring nothing in that wasn't going to belong to everybody. Esther, bless her heart, got the idea somewhere that she needed to have something for herself. I think that's why she got pregnant. She musta really been blinded by lust and selfishness to think that a child could come into our home and not be shared. Hezekiah was born on Christmas morning, and believe you me, he was the best present we ever had. Course that preacher didn't marry my sister, but she didn't want him to. Good thing, 'cause my daddy would've brought that man in front of our church himself and told folks what he did if Mama hadn't stepped in.

"Think on what is good," she told Daddy late one night. "We gonna have another baby in the house, and you know how that make me feel."

Now, we could hear most everything that went on in our three-bedroom house, so I knew that my daddy ain't need to be told nothing else. Folks nowadays don't like to think of they parents doing the do. But we use to laugh and giggle whenever we heard the headboard banging and slats falling from under they old bed.

"Mama and Daddy are making happy," my younger sister, Olivia, use to say. Those were good times. We ain't have much, but we never went hungry. And we had a house full of love.

Lord, I done talked myself all 'round the barn again just to tell you why I had a hard time when me and Jim first got married. It was the first time I was in a place that wasn't filled with talk and laughter. I tried to fill in all the emptiness by talking 'bout anything. Jim would smile his pulled-back smile, the one that didn't show his teeth. I came to know that that smile was really Jim laughing at me.

"Woman, can't we just enjoy the quiet?"

I use to think, "What in the world is enjoyable about quiet?"

I kept right on talking, and Jim kept on smiling that pulled-back smile. When it came to me that he was really laughing at me, I got all pouty and told him if something were to happen to me and I couldn't talk, he sure would miss my voice then. Well, Jim took me by the hand and led me out of that little place on B Street that we first lived in. When I tried to ask where we were going, he said, "Hush up woman, and don't say nothing." You know that didn't stop me, but whenever I tried to get in a word, Jim would give me a look that said he was really meaning for me to stay quiet. We walked over to Old Man Wilson's, who lived only a few doors down.

Jim say, "Stay here and don't say nothing."

Now, I was getting scared, 'cause we were newly married, and I was thinking that maybe I married somebody with more than one personality. Jim went inside, but was only there for a few minutes. He came back out with the keys to Mr. Wilson's car. We ain't had our own when we first got married, which really made us appreciate when we did and every one after it. I feel sorry for my children and most of you young folks who think you gotta have everything before you can start to live. Life is not in the stuff. Because Jim and I worked together to build this life, we can take our time enjoying it. When you rush into something, you end up rushing out. That goes for most everything, rushing into getting stuff will help you lose it.

Anyway, Jim borrowed Mr. Wilson's car and told me to get in and don't talk. Now, I wanted to laugh, but I ain't know if that was considered talking, so I didn't. Jim drove me all through our little town and then out to the country. Now, getting to the country when you live in a country town ain't a long trip. But I gotta tell you true, it seemed like the longest ride of my life. I had never knowed how talking could make time fly by. That's when it dawned on me, that it took away something else too. It took away the details of life. There were things I saw that day that I had never seen before. I thought I knew that town like I knew the back of my hand. Turns out I only knew it like the back of my head. I could feel my way around, but I hadn't really seen it up close. Jim took me to the little place where he had asked me to marry him. I always thought of it as our place. There was a stream that flowed down onto some rocks and a beautiful pasture. Outside of that wasn't much I could have told you. But in my silence, I saw the trees. They were blooming and busting with life. There were woodpeckers, squirrels, little gophers, and all kinds of ants, moving back and forth, working like it was joy. That's when it came to me that work should be joy. I saw the way some grass seemed to stand straight, but some like to lay over. It was all in the thickness. The thicker that grass, the straighter it stood. Then I saw the richness of what I thought of as dirt. I could smell it too. I sit down, and Jim do the same. I look at that dirt for some time, and then I dug into it and let it clump and break between my fingers. Something told me to taste it, and I do. I was surprised at how much it reminded me of fresh ground coffee with chickory, but there was something more. It taste like everything you might need. I thought I was losing it for a second and turn around to see Jim stretched out on his back, staring up at the sky.

"Woman," he say, disturbing what I now think of as *my* silence, "I would rather be here with you in silence than hear anything else again in life."

I ain't say nothing. Jim kissed me on the forehead and

pulled me up from my peace. "Come on, dirt eater," he said, laughing. We went back to our place in silence and stay that way for the rest of the day. I can still get my talk on, as one of my grandbabies likes to say, but I have learned the power of silence. I'd been thinking on all that I'm telling you when I finally remembered Jim's question.

"What do you think we are supposed to do with all this love?" I ask in response to what Jim had asked many thoughts before.

Jim turned to me and smiled. "I love the way you think. I never could see how you jumped from one point to another. Now it all makes sense."

It only took a second to understand that Jim had followed me in my thinking.

"This surely is as good as it is hard, ain't it, baby?" I ask him.

"Sure is," he said.

He gave me that pulled-back smile of his, 'cause he now knew all that it meant to me. We both laughed.

"Well," Jim say, "nothing is ever given to you for you alone. All that we are and have is to be shared with others."

"Amen. Amen," I tell him.

Now, my Jim was a man of God. He showed it with his life, not his words. He couldn't stand a lot of what he called "emotion preachers." Those were the ministers who played on folks' feelings. Sometimes, if a preacher came through who really rubbed Jim the wrong way, he would refer to them as the "hit it and quit it" type. Now, Jim never said this to me. I happened to overhear him talking with my brothers and brothers-in-love one day when we got together to remember my parents' life. We never celebrated they birthdays or the anniversaries of they deaths. That would've made both of them get up and haunt us if they could've. ⚊

Instead, from time to time whenever the mood hit, we got together to talk about they lives and the legacy they had left us in they words and deeds. The men had all ended up out in the backyard, telling jokes that the children shouldn't hear and were just being who they were when women weren't around. I know now that there's a huge difference, only because of this hearing thing that done come on me. But back then, when I heard Jim saying that the preacher just "hit it and quit it," I was wondering where my sweet husband had learned such a thing.

"They come in here, get folks all worked up, take they money, and leave."

"Seem like that preacher could've at least took me to dinner first," I heard my brother, Bubby, say.

They all laughed and rocked back so far in them folding chairs that I thought they might break. Seem like they had all practiced that move, 'cause them chairs came forward all together like the usher board taking up the collection.

"Woman, I ever tell you you got a way with words?" Jim ask me all a sudden.

"Get out of my head," I tell him.

I finally got up from where I was laying, even though I did not want to. But Jim was right: Stewardship is not about how well we take care of something, it's about how well we share it. At that moment though, I came to understand how folks could just lay around on a Sunday and think about what they had and how they was gonna get more. I could see why folks felt like going to work and coming home was all they needed to do, and why people live and die not having an impact on anything or anyone around them. 'Cause living for self can get comfortable, not comfortable in the true sense, like satisfaction, but comfortable like in "this is all I need to do, want to do, feel like doing." I got up and pulled the blankets off the bed.

"Girl, what you doing now?" Jim ask like he didn't know. "I know. I know, but I gotta learn to act like I don't."

"Help me with this," I say for both our hearing.

We commence to cleaning that house like it had never been clean. My grandmother told me when I was still a girl and was complaining about my chores, that work is healing. "You got a problem? Clean from one corner of the house to the other, and everything will be clear when it's all clean."

Jim always fixed things and helped me to keep things straight, especially after the kids was grown and gone, but he never really did the deep cleaning. But bless my soul, he cleaned like my grandma use to. He got caught up in it so that it looked like cleaning was his reason for living. He swept, mopped, and then waxed the hardwood floors in each room. He cleaned baseboards and walls while I worked on cleaning light fixtures and windows. I polished down the furniture, which is real different from dusting. Dusting is really just a wipe-off, but polishing is a good rubdown. Jim cleaned the outside of the windows, while I did the inside. We scrubbed our house good on the inside and then got to working on the outside. I swept the porch and sidewalk, and Jim hosed them down. Miss Brown came out on her porch and waved at us. She was squinting and trying to figure out what we'd been up to. I saw Jim snicker when we both heard her thinking that we must have been real sick to have to clean the house like that. She hadn't seen us doing our daily routine for three days, and then when we did come out, it was to clean. Right then, Jim took that hose and squirted me with it and started laughing. The front of me was all soaked. Jim let me catch him and turn the hose on him before I realized that his little show was for Miss Brown.

"They sure have been acting strange," she was thinking. "I bet they done hit the lottery and getting ready to move."

"Louella," Jim whispered, "make sure you dig up all the money 'fore we go."

He was laughing so hard that I had to laugh with him. I somehow got caught in the hose and tripped and fell. Jim was laughing the whole time.

"What am I gonna do with this woman?" Jim say for Miss Brown's hearing.

That's when we felt the pain of her loneliness. I'ma tell you true, sometimes we so busy reacting to what we think people do to us, that we don't ever think about what's been done to them. Miss Brown was by far the nosiest person I had ever met. She the kind of person who knew everything about everybody, but no one knew a thing about her. She was a watcher, but not much of a talker. She didn't go no place, and with the exception of her son who visited once every two or three years, no one came to see her. She looked at me and Jim and wondered where her life had gone. Then she just turned around and went back inside.

I wanted to go to her right then, but I knew Miss Brown would need some time. When we first moved to our home on Elm Street, which by the way we now own free and clear, we were greeted by almost everybody except Miss Brown. Now, in a small town like this one, most folks already know who everybody is anyway. The greeting and giving of baked goods was just a way to say "Welcome to the street." That's why I was shocked when I found out that I had neighbors I didn't know. I thought everybody there was raised the same way I was. Anyway, I used to see Miss Brown watching me and Jim through her curtains, so I went over to introduce myself and took her a pound cake. Bible says, "If you wanna make friends, you gotta show yourself friendly." I didn't want to have a neighbor who was watching us but not liking us. It wouldn't been good for my kids. Anyway, when I took her that cake, she opened the door and looked at me like I was blocking her view.

"What you want?" she say with her hand on her hip. I tried to introduce myself when she said, "I knew you when you were a girl playing in mud. Don't come over here, trying to act grown, Louella Givens. Oh excuse me—Johnson. I know you and the dirt that made you. Take whatever mess it is you got under that foil and get off my porch."

Now, I was raised right, so I know to respect my elders, but something in me wanted to pound that woman with that pound cake. But just 'cause she don't know good cooking don't mean it gotta go to waste. I must have stared at her for a whole minute before she say, "What's wrong with you, gal? Can't you hear? Get off my porch and go be grown somewhere else."

I left before I had the chance to ignore my upbringing. On my way back across the street, Mr. Wilson called me over.

"Don't pay that no mind," he say. "She's like everybody else. She has good days and bad days, just her bad one's are real bad. Go back over there tomorrow. She'll wave to you like it never happened."

The very next day, Miss Brown, true to whatever ailed her, was standing on the porch waving. I waved back, but I didn't want to. I was thinking on all of that when I noticed that Jim was crying.

"How can folks expect to heal when they keep digging at old wounds?" Jim was meaning Miss Brown and me.

I would have felt some shame, but I knew that shame was the blister that came from digging at old wounds.

"How do folks live without loving?" Jim ask as he made his way back into our house.

"Well," I say, following him, "I suspect that's the reason why we got this gift. To help people out."

# CHAPTER SEVEN

# Sick and Tired of Being Tired

*I*t's true: Life's problems are like a scab on a wound. You keep picking, they can't heal. Some folks scratch it 'cause it feels good to them. That's when it starts to bleed again. Well, I told you 'bout my old neighbor, Mae, the one that was all up in my business back when me and Jim first got married and lived over on B Street. Well, Mae still over in that same apartment, living the same kinda life. She came over after she hadn't seen me nor Jim around town for three days. In small towns like ours everybody gets to know everybody else's routine.

"Yoo-hoo," she yelled in through the screen door.

Before she could even wait for an answer, I heard the door pull the half inch of give, then slap back shut. Jim had put up a hook and latch on account of folks like Mae and Lucy, people who don't wait for an invitation to come in. From them old black-and-white horror movies that come on late at night, I can see that even vampires got more manners than Lucy and Mae.

"Who's pulling my door, trying to break in?" I say in that annoying acting-like-I'm-being-nice-but-ain't voice.

That Dr. Phil, who come on *Oprah,* calls them people like Mae "passive aggressives." I just call them a nuisance. Still, I like the way he deal with them uppity city folks with his degrees and the common sense his mama gave him. I really love the way Oprah stares at them crazy folks and say, "Dr. Phil, is this, uh, normal?" That cracks me up, 'cause she know them folks are nutty. But she let the doctor who's white and a man say it so folks will keep on tuning in. "Gone girl," I say to that TV. Now, don't get to thinking that I done gone back to watching TV all day. Truth is, I hardly ever watch. Sometimes though, when I'm visiting my children, I try to act as old as they treat me, so I sit around and do nothing. They think I'm old, so I let them cook and clean. Anyway, Mae was standing at the door when I walked around from the kitchen.

"Hey, girl," I say in that same aggressive-on-the-sly voice.

"Your door is locked, Louella."

Now I'm thinking, *Who you think locked it?* but I ain't say it.

"Well, I do declare," I say instead. "I'm just trying to keep the devil out. You wouldn't be the devil, would you?"

"No," she say, kinda impatient like. "But if I was, you know that little hook wouldn't keep me out. Them little thieving niggers that run up and down your street can get into anything, lock or no."

I unhook the lock to let Mae in, but God knows I ain't want to. It's amazing to me how folks can find everybody's sin but they own. I really don't take to folks calling my children out of they name. Black kids got enough to worry about just trying to grow up. The last thing they need is an old Black person calling them by the same name they ancestors were called. True, them children do call each other "nigger," but that's 'cause they learn it from older folks who never learned to respect theyselves. Since she's in my house, I decide to tell her just that.

"Now, Mae, I don't need no old, pissy furniture."

I wait for her to look at me like she think I'm crazy, and she did, so I tell her what I mean.

"The word 'nigger' is like an old, nasty piece of furniture that somebody wants to put in your house. At first we say, 'No thank you, I have a nice place already,' but then somebody convince us that all we have to do is fix up a bit, make it look a little different. 'Cause we ain't been told no better, we go right ahead and bring that old, nasty, pissy sofa inside. Now, Mae Verne Prescott, there ain't no niggers 'round here. But how you been, girl?" I throw in real quick.

I like to change the subject on folks so they don't get a chance to feel no lower 'bout theyself than is necessary. Mae got to blinking like something's in her eye, and I check to see if my hand is still attached to my wrist. My mama use to tell us kids, "It's better to slap somebody with the truth than with your hand. Your hand can't change the way they think."

"I'm fine," Mae said, still confused.

"Sit down girl. Can I get you some lemonade or maybe some iced tea?"

"That would be nice," she say.

Now I want to slap myself. I was always taught to be neighborly, but there's some folks you just don't like getting too comfortable. Mae's one of them.

"Which do you prefer?" I ask her.

"Whatever is made," she say, getting up to follow me into the kitchen.

You can ask any good cook to see if I'm telling you true. We don't like folks standing over us in our kitchen. Anything that's real takes a lot of private preparation. Take Pastor DuBois. He can preach. He don't do that hopping and hollering that most folks seem to like. He don't use a long string of fancy words that weren't ever meant to go together neither. He teach the truth like God said it. I find him very powerful, so I know that a lot of private study and prayer went into each one of them sermons.

My children are all wonderful. They got they faults and shortcomings just like anybody else, but they good people with real good hearts. Now, not all five of them was planned, but a lot of private preparation went into each one of them. I know as sure as I know my name, that every one of them was made on nights when me and Jim were at our best. I love every one of them and wouldn't trade them for nothing, but I sure do wish me and Jim knew then what we know now.

Anyway, Mae follow me into the kitchen and sat down at one of the benches into my breakfast nook. Jim made it for me with his own hands and a lot of love. It's got bright yellow and orange flowers on a white background that stay white 'cause I give it a good scrubbing every two weeks. The bench part is made from oak. It's painted white, and it's real clean too. Jim made the table from the same kind of wood but added formica on the top. I'm proud of all the things Jim made, but something 'bout that bright set that makes my heart skip. It's one of the first pieces we had. Most folks would've throw it out by now. My son Larry, bless his mixed-up heart, tried to get me a brand-new, store-bought set to replace it. He came down here with his high-yellow wife, whose color I only mention because she would want me to. Black folks got people of every color somewhere in they family, but they get caught up on one end or the other. I got children who only like them real light and others who only like them real dark. If you ask me, and I know you didn't, they all crazy. Color don't make you pretty. Who you be do. Anyway, Larry, my son, came down here to visit 'bout three summers ago. I do believe I heard his sister say that he had to buy his wife the new car they was driving in exchange for getting to visit. She whispered to him how he should help us out and fix up the place. I even heard her offer to decorate. My son got a funny look on his face, but didn't say nothing 'cause he's his daddy's chile. She convince him to at least get a new kitchen set. Well, my son take me to the furniture store and tell me to pick out what I think I want. He musta been looking at those new, big ole TVs that's too big to see good, 'cause he didn't notice when I walked on out of that store. He was walking up and down the aisles for some time 'fore he realized I was gone. When he finally made his way back home, I had already made dinner. Me and Jim was eating at that same table he wanted to get rid of. He came in and smell that good food, look and see his mama and daddy loving each other more than when we first met, and knew why that table would never go. He took his wife to the hotel she insisted on staying at. Now, I can't say for sure, 'cause I wasn't there, but I'd love to been a fly on that wall, 'cause when they came back the next day, that woman was grinning like I never seen and so was my boy. I suspect she got a good talking to and some good loving to seal the deal.

Anyway, Mae decided on iced tea after all. I guess 'cause it wasn't already made, and some folks like to have stuff done for them even though they wouldn't do it for themself. It makes them feel important. Anyhow, I fix the tea with peppermint leaves and lemon and end up warming up the leftovers from the night before. Mae tell me that my leftovers are the only ones she will eat. I'm thinking to myself that she sure got some nerve. I wouldn't eat her food if it just came off the stove. But as my grandson would say, "Ain't no need for her to hate. She should just appreciate or congratulate." Something like that.

From the moment Mae walked in, I can feel a sadness around her. I saw that her life had been one big, revolving door. Men were coming and going so fast, she hardly had time to know herself. Now that she was getting up in age, that steady flow of men had slowed down to a trickle. Most of Mae's men were married. Whatever it had been that had attracted them to her didn't last. They stayed where they had roots, not where they had been picking flowers. Mae would have never admitted it to me, probably not even to herself, but she was lonely. All the attention she got back when she was young wasn't coming her way no more. She was never beautiful, but she had that way that could stop a man in his tracks. Mae wasn't that small, but she wasn't fat neither. She was tall and thick in the top, but small in the bottom. She always had large breasts, but she never saw the need for a bra. Gravity got a way of telling you what you should've done. Mae always wore bright colors and lots of makeup and perfume. She wore all kinds of wigs and hair pieces too. She wasn't at all tacky though. Mae knew how to put it together, and she knew how to dress so she made the not so good parts look great and the great parts look that much better. But as Mae got older and her pool of rent-paying boyfriends started to dry up, she had to make do with what she had. Taking care of your outside and ignoring the inside didn't help Mae's aging process none either. It's a sad thing when pretty women spend their whole life trying to be pretty and then have to watch it fade away. That's what was going on with Mae.

"You looking good, Miss Mae," I say, trying to ease the pain she would never claim. She blush a bit like she done trained herself to do.

"How that fine husband of yours?" she ask, needing something to be the object of her attention other than me.

"He fine as always," I tell her.

"You hit the jackpot with that man, girl." Mae is getting ready to be as nice as she can. "Your man is a good man. You know I done been with a few in my day. One thing you can say for Jim Johnson, he never strayed much."

There it was, the knife she always hid in the roses.

"Mae, seem like you can't be nice without trying to hurt somebody," I tell her right out.

"I just tell the truth, and you know that. I don't lie to nobody for nothing."

She was flipping her false lashes like they were new. They were as old as the mascara that was caked up on them.

"Then why do you lie to yourself?" I ask her.

Mae had more sense than I gave her credit for. She didn't get mad or try to answer right away. She sat there as proud as she could and looked me dead in the eyes. You could really cut the tension in that little kitchen. I ain't say nothing either 'cause the Bible say that with many words, you offend much. There was a whole lot I could have told Mae about herself, but I had already done a lot with that one question.

I could hear Mae thinking all that she wanted to tell me. I heard her saying that she could've had Jim if she wanted to. Then I heard her admit that she had tried her best, but Jim wasn't the least bit interested. I watched as she remembered finding out that Jim had been unfaithful to me and hisself with a woman from Marysville. Then I watched that smile leave when I told her that I knew all about it.

"You ain't thinking nothing that I don't already know, Miss Mae," I tell her.

Well, I guess that was one word too many. Mae turn a funny gray that somehow showed through all that makeup she had on.

"How you know what I'm thinking, Louella? What you done messed with?"

Mae was thinking I was into roots or something. She had to feel that way, since I know that she's into root work herself. Don't get me wrong, I know that there is much more to this life than we can see or feel. I'm a living witness to that fact, but some folks done fooled themselves into believing that they can control someone else's will with they own. I already told you how I wouldn't ever eat none of Mae's food. Well, there's a reason besides her bad cooking. Mae has been known to add a few unsavory things to her pot every now and then.

"You know I don't work no roots, but God works in mysterious ways, his wonders to perform."

"Fine, then what am I thinking now?" she say, challenging me like I'm one of her married men she's threatening to expose.

"I ain't got nothing to prove to you, Mae. You came

here 'cause you in pain. You lonely. You like the peace that real love brings around me and my family. You want it, but you want to destroy it just the same. I can't tell you what to do with your life, but I can tell you to stop messing in mine.

"Now this thing fall on me and Jim. I done seen more sadness than I care to. Love brings about joy, but empty sex doesn't bring you nothing but emptiness."

Mae commence to crying, just like Mr. Blue and Mr. Stan.

"I'm tired, Louella," she say. "I'm just tired."

"Why you tired?" I ask her.

I do this 'cause I know that Mae got the answers to her own problems, but she gotta look on the inside of them for herself.

"I'm just tired. I done lived like I was in a race. Everything was 'bout having a good time. I didn't save nothing for now."

Since ain't nobody in our little town got a whole lot of anything, I can tell that Mae ain't talking 'bout money. She talking 'bout herself. She ain't store up no memories or no love. Empty sex don't give you long-lasting memories. It don't give you peace during difficult times. It only last for the moment that you having them. Mae ain't got none of life's goodness put away, and somehow she thinks that putting other folks down will give her some kind of happiness.

"I don't mean you no harm, Louella. I never have. I guess I just wish I had what you have. Always did."

I tried to give her some kind of smile 'cause the way out she looking for ain't nothing that's gonna happen real quick. Everything is a process.

"How you want to live the rest of your life?" I ask Mae.

I can tell right away that she been giving that a whole lot of thought. I can also tell that she hurting more than I thought. Then she said what I heard in one quick flash, "I'm dying, Louella."

Soon as she say it out loud, I can see the torment that's raging in her body. I see what they call cancer and other kinds of nastiness that shouldn't be there.

"I'm sorry," I tell her, 'cause I really am.

"I ain't got nothing to call my own. I have nothing to leave that's gonna mean anything. I don't know why I'm telling you this, Louella. I was gonna come over and see if you and Jim was okay. Somebody said they hadn't seen y'all for days. You the talk of the town, girl," Mae said, trying to smile. "I see you here looking real good, like you younger or something."

"That's just good loving," I tell her.

Mae start back to looking sad again.

"What you want for the rest of your life?" I ask again.

Mae looked up at the ceiling like that answer might fall through it. She sat that way for a while, so I went on and baked some of them biscuits of mine that she loves so much. I brewed some fresh coffee while Mae sat there, thinking back on her life. It wasn't 'til those biscuits came out of the oven that Mae was able to talk about what it was that she needed.

"I want what you have, Louella, real love."

She cried some more, and this time I joined her. I took Mae in my arms and rocked her like she was my own baby.

"Love ain't something you get unless it's something you give," I tell her. "You show love to others, then you see it all around you."

I heard Mae thinking that that's why she dying, on account of she done give herself to too many people.

"Not your body, Mae, yourself, who you are. You got to love with that."

Mae stared at me real hard. "Since when you get the gift, Louella Johnson?" she ask.

"It's a long story, and you wouldn't believe it if I told you, Mae. Just take it when I tell you that it's a joy and a pain, but it's real."

"How did I throw my life away, and this plain old woman end up with so much?" Mae ask herself.

As soon as she did, she look at me and say she sorry.

"No need to apologize," I tell her. "It ain't like you said it to hurt me. You just thought it to yourself. I was the one all up in your head with my plain old self."

This time Mae laughed a big ole, happy laugh. I knew

just then that she was gonna be a real friend. After Mae ate enough biscuits to bust and she filled me in on things that I didn't need to know, she said she was gonna go on home. She broke down and cried again.

"I'm being evicted, Louella," she say.

Just then, Jim came in and proved again what a wonderful man he is.

"Mae Verne Prescott, what you and my wife down here going on so much for?"

Mae tried to fix herself up, 'cause I guess old habits really do die hard.

"Hey, Jim Johnson, you still fine, I see. I was about to ask your wife to loan me some money 'til I can see my way clear," she say, feeling more comfortable around us than she ever had before.

"You don't need to pay that no good landlord another dime or nothing else," Jim say.

Everybody in town knew that Mae had two ways to pay for things: with her body, and with money she got from using her body. I guess neither one was working too well for her no more.

"You can stay right here for as long as you need to."

Jim said that and went right back upstairs to whatever he had been doing.

"Well, Mae," I say, "you heard the man."

"I can't just move in here. What's folks gonna say?

You know what I am. I don't need to burden y'all with this. Besides I ain't . . ."

"I know," I tell her. "You ain't never really like me that much. You just loved me 'cause you wanted to be like me."

Then I did something I hadn't done for years. I stuck my tongue out at Mae, grabbed her by the hand, and we skipped all the way to her little apartment, laughing like girls. Anybody that saw us had to think we done lost our minds.

# CHAPTER EIGHT

# The Road to Heaven

*I*f I hadn't felt sad enough for Mae before, I really felt it when I went into that little place she called home. I will never be able to understand how some folks can spend all they life and time dressing up theyself, but living and sleeping in filth. Mae was not a clean woman. I don't know if she had been this way her whole life, 'cause I was never much for running in and out of other folks' houses, but it seem like she had never bothered to look up under anything. She just kept piling more on.

"Lord, woman, this place is gonna take days to clean out."

"Fine, then my funky-behind landlord can do it. I ain't got nothing worth keeping or giving away."

Mae grabbed a bag that was already packed. I guess that's how she had been living and said, "Let's go."

"What about the rest of this?" I ask her.

"Like I said, I ain't got nothing in here that mean anything."

We walked back to my house, but being in her place took all the skip out of our step. I didn't say nothing on the way back, 'cause there wasn't nothing that could say what I felt. We got home and I set Mae and her little bag of things up in the room Jim had built over our garage. Our youngest son, Neal, had stayed there for a year after he finished what he called "undergraduate studies." Seem to me he always graduating from some school. He's working on his last degree now and is gonna finish this year. Jim done already told him that he can't come back though.

"With all them degrees, you ought to be able to control the weather," Jim tell him.

But I know my man. He so proud, he can bust. "My boy gonna be something," he say to me one night. "We just don't know yet what it is."

Mae looked around that makeshift apartment and just smiled. It was real clean and bright. My son, who is studying how to think about stuff, is real good at painting. He painted the walls to look like a park, and practically everything else in there look like it belong in a park. The chair look like a big rock. The bed is painted with roses all over the headboard. Even the curtains are painted. The ceiling look like a sky, and them curtains got kites all over them that lead up into the walls. I'm a tell the truth and shame the devil. When that boy first brought me up there and told me when I could open my eyes, I wanted to whoop his behind for painting up my stuff like he was crazy.

"You done gone to school so long that you come back dumb," I tell him.

"It's a park," he say, grinning. "I brought the outside in."

"Why didn't you just move outside?" I say.

He laughed and said a bunch of big words I ain't a bit more understand than I did his so-called apartment. Now standing here with this woman who had lived her whole life trying to find love, but getting nothing but pain, I saw all the beauty that boy had created.

Mae cried some more and hugged me for the first time since I knew her. She was about to say thank you, when I told her that she didn't have to.

"Be at peace, and I'll have all the thanks I need."

I left Mae in that room and went to find the only man who had ever eased this woman's burdens. When I got back over to the house, I saw that Jim was sitting in our kitchen, eating a biscuit.

"Hmm, Jim James Johnson, what's everybody gonna say when they find out you got Mae Prescott living in your house?"

Jim looked up and smiled his pulled-back smile.

"They gonna say that Jim is one lucky man. He got himself two women."

I grabbed the tea towel and popped Jim with it like I used to do the kids. He laughed and smacked me on the behind.

"Don't start nothing you can't finish," I say, walking past Jim.

Jim took one of my breasts in his hand and put his mouth on the other one.

"When I do finish, woman, you gonna beg me to start again," he said between sucking and biting.

"Umm, I love you, man," I tell him.

"You better," he whispered in my ear. " 'Cause if you don't, I can go right up over that garage and get my other wife to give me what I need."

I laughed and pulled away from Jim. He pulled me right back.

"Pull them blinds down, woman. You don't want to make my other wife jealous, do you?"

"Not here, Jim. I gotta cook in this kitchen, and I don't want to have to find hairs on the table or on my counter."

Jim let out one of his big laughs.

"You too clean for my own good," Jim said.

That's when I got to really get joy out of my breakfast

nook. Jim sat me down and pulled the bench out away from the table.

"Don't scratch up my floor," I yelled.

"Sit down, woman," Jim told me.

I did as I was told and was so glad I did. Jim pulled up my dress and pulled my panties off. He folded them up and put them in the back pocket of his jeans.

"See, no mess on your floor," he say, looking up into my eyes.

Jim kissed my toe and worked up to my ankle. He nibbled at my calf and then kneaded the inside and tops of my thighs. I forgot all about what I was leaking onto my little kitchenette and enjoyed the flow of my happiness. Jim stuck his finger up into me while he licked the outside of me.

"Yes," I tell him. "Do it just like that."

Jim smiled and stood up for a second. I thought he was gonna leave. He heard my thought and started laughing.

"I couldn't leave now if I tried," I heard him say in my head.

Jim unzipped his pants and let them fall to his ankles. All that we had been doing still didn't take away the feeling we were kids sneaking candy before dinner or something.

Jim smiled and said, "This is candy, woman. I'm

gonna give you some, and you gonna give me some back."

I giggled and just when I did, Jim pulled my right leg up higher than I even knew I could go.

"Give this to me, woman," he say right up in my ear.

Jim grabbed my behind and pushed inside me. He pulled back slowly and pushed in hard.

"I will always love you. I will love you when what we're doing is a memory. I will love you when I can't hear or see you. I will think of this every time I come in this kitchen, and in my heart I will come again just like I'm coming now."

When he said this, he came so hard that I came right with him. But my Jim wasn't done. He pulled out of me and sucked Miss Lou 'til I kept right on coming.

"This is the sweetest pussy in the world," Jim said when he was done.

I cried 'cause I couldn't think of nothing else to do, then I cried again 'cause I thought of Mae out across our little backyard up in that garage with nobody to love her like Jim was loving me.

"Everybody makes the bed they lay in," Jim say.

I stopped crying, and me and Jim went to our own bed and slept the sadness off.

The next morning Jim beat me getting up. When I didn't find him next to me or in the bathroom, I followed the smell of PineSol into the kitchen and found him there cleaning the floor. The seats from my breakfast nook were outside airing out. Jim was humming and working like it was nothing but joy.

"You finally got up huh, lazy bones?" he say, playing.

"I can tell it's gonna be a long weekend 'round here," I said.

"Well it ought to be cause it's been one heck of a week."

I made some fresh coffee and heated up the biscuits from the night before. I fried Jim some eggs and made turkey sausages. We don't eat pork no more on account of what my son told me. Naim is his new name, but I still call him Neal. He don't mind either. But he do mind if we don't respect his eating habits. He showed us how lots of the food that we came up on is killing our bodies. Since then, I use turkey or chicken, which he says I'll have to work myself out of. I told you my kids can be kinda crazy. Well, he one of them. Anyway, when I make that breakfast, Mae come down like it was an alarm.

"Something sure do smell good."

I get to thinking that Mae is still Mae, and when I do she say she can't stay for breakfast.

"I need to get over to the doctor's office for my medication and checkup. Then I'm gonna go see if I can volunteer somewhere." I look at her to see if she okay, and commence to laughing.

"Don't look at me like that, Miss Louella. It may be

hard to believe, but I sat up all night thinking of how I'm gonna get my love. Well, I know that the church is looking for volunteers at the day care, and I'm gonna see if I can help out."

"How you know that, Mae?" I ask her.

She do that close-to-blushing thing she does and say that she know some of the folks over at Calvary Temple. I know she mean menfolks, but I just tell her to go on with her bad self. I wanted to tell her to take off some of her makeup and find a dress that ain't show so much cleavage, but I ain't want to hurt her feelings on her first day of newness. Besides, I thought to myself, that church sure should be happy to see her come in there. Many good members had slipped a bit on their way to heaven by stopping at Mae Prescott's house.

Mae left happy, but she ain't come back that way.

"Them no good sons of a—'scuse me," Mae say. "I know you a decent woman so I need to watch my mouth, but them no good dogs at that church had the nerve to tell me they ain't want me 'round none of they kids. That older heifer, Letha, laughed right in my face when I told her why I was there. Just 'cause she been in the church all her life don't mean that the church been in her. I happen to know that them first and last girls of hers didn't come from her husband. And don't let me get started on her husband, Cleophus. That man's dick ain't—"

"Alright Mae," I say, trying to calm her down. "Don't

worry none 'bout what nobody got to say. You know who you are and what you been doing better than they do. And you know how you feel about it. Church folks ain't never had the market on righteous living. They human like everybody else."

*What I'm gonna do?* Mae asks herself. *I can't go in that church on Sunday.*

I heard her thinking through her plans to give her life to God on the coming Sunday and could tell how much it meant to her.

"God ain't in the church, Mae," I tell her. "He's in us. You want to accept him, you can do it right here."

That's when I found out 'bout who Mae Prescott really was.

"I know the Lord. I accepted Jesus as my savior and teacher back when I was a girl. I have read the word every day of my life. I didn't grow up 'round here. I'm from outside of Memphis. My daddy was a preacher and my mama was a traveling evangelist. They did a lot of real good work, but somebody didn't want them doing it. They had Blacks and Whites at they meetings, and I guess back then it was too much for folks to take. They hung my daddy and my mama from the tree right in front of our house. Only reason they didn't kill me was because by the time they got through doing what they wanted to do to me, some of the members had come to our defense. It was too late for my mama and daddy, and in a way it was too late for me. I lived with my aunt and uncle 'til they saw I was just too much to handle. That's when I came over here. I been here for so long, most folks just think I belong here. That's what happens when your living is a mess, it seems to be bigger than it really is."

Believe me when I tell you, everybody got a story. I just never ever thought that Mae's would be so sad. If I had thought about it long enough though, I would have realized that the sadder the life, the sadder the story behind it. Trouble don't make itself.

"Well, Mae," I say through my heavy heart, "then you know the Lord. All you need to do is walk in His goodness. What did Jesus say to the woman that all them men wanted to stone to death 'cause of her adultery?"

"He said, let he who is without sin cast the first stone," Mae say.

I had to tell myself not to act surprised.

"That's right girl. Now you know that half the folks with stones in they hand had a way in making that woman what she was."

"Mae, it's just you and me sitting here, so I'ma ask you like Jesus ask that woman, where are your accusers?"

Mae smile a little, but them tears was steady flowing. "You got a lot of life to give Mae. Besides, there's plenty of work for you to do."

"Like what?" Mae ask, looking at me like I'm crazy.

"Well, you tell me, Mae."

Mae start to laugh, and I had to laugh with her. She was thinking of all them things she did to the men of our little town and how she could not go around doing that for Jesus.

"I know the word say whatever you do, to do it as unto God, but I don't think he want me going around giving out dick-sucking lessons."

We laughed so hard, I 'bout peed my pants.

"Lord, Louella, if somebody had told me I'd be in your house, laughing about all kinds of mess, I would have told them to go back to the nut farm they came from. God sure do work in miraculous ways," she say.

"Sure do," I say back to her.

Mae helped me cook dinner by tasting everything and telling me it was good. She said she wasn't much for cooking or cleaning.

"We gonna find your other talent, girl. You just wait."

That night, before Mae went back to her new living space, she thanked me and Jim again.

"I know that you all are from God, and so is this new gift you got, 'cause ain't no way you old goats could get it on like you did last night if it wasn't."

As dark as my Jim is, he still turned red as a berry. It came to me then that we didn't pull down the blinds like we intend to. But before I could worry too much, Mae said, "Don't turn too red, Jim. I like to show, but I ain't one for watching. Soon as I see y'all carrying on, I closed my own blinds. You just better hope the rest of your neighbors did the same. Good night y'all. I'll see you in the morning, God willing."

Jim looked at me and we laughed so hard that night, we could hardly stop. When the laughter died down, Jim would start up all over again. It really got funny when I made Jim go out back to see whether he could see our breakfast nook from outside. He came back laughing harder than when he left.

"The only house that has a good view is Miss Brown's," he said, laughing. "We better check up on her tomorrow, make sure she ain't have no heart attack or nothing. Good thing we had the door shut, or she would have heard you crying for your mama."

I punched Jim's arm, and he hugged me real tight.

"Good night, woman. I hope that shows you not to beg for it in the kitchen no more."

I punched Jim again and laughed myself to sleep.

When I got to sleep that night, my grandmother was there smiling.

"You doing real good," she said. "You done learned that love is for sharing. Keep this up, and you gonna be as popular as your friend, Mae."

She was gone before I had a chance to ask her what she meant.

The next morning was Sunday, and Jim and I got

ready for church like we always do. We both wondered if we should bother with inviting Mae, but by the time we got downstairs, she was dressed and ready. She had on a lot less makeup than I had ever seen her wear. Her dress was still one of her low-cut numbers, but Mae had found one of my son's old, long-sleeve shirts and had it on up under that dress.

"I know I look a little tacky," she say. "But can't nobody say I came in with my stuff hanging out. I would've made breakfast, but you know I can't cook, so I just waited for y'all."

Jim had tears in the corners of his eyes, which made her tear up too. I fixed a quick breakfast of cheese grits, eggs, and hash browns. I call this "Neal's vegetarian breakfast" even though he tells me it's too much starch and that eggs are chicken embryos. I told that boy to shut up and eat. Mae and Jim ate while I started on Sunday dinner. It's hard to break the habits I had when my children were all here. I used to have so many mouths to feed that I did what my mama always did: prepare as much as possible before church. That way you didn't have all of your day's work staring you in the face at one time.

When we went out to get into our car, we were greeted by Miss Brown from across the street. She was on her porch waving all happy like. I figured she was having one of her good days and was glad for it.

"Morning, Mae. Morning, Louella, Jim," she say. "Y'all got room for one more?" she ask.

Now, I'ma tell you the only way I know. I ain't never know Miss Brown to go to nobody's church. I think it was too regular for her irregularities.

"Sure," Jim say, like this was normal.

He heard my thoughts and looked at me hard.

"Expect a whole lot to change, woman," he tell my mind.

When Miss Brown came off her porch, she was moving like she was ten years younger than her age. She was humming some tune and grinning. She grabbed hold of Mae's hand like Mae was her little girl or something. Mae held right back like it was natural, and we got in the car as if we'd been doing this every Sunday. What happened next was what my grandmama had been trying to prepare me for the night before in my sleep. If I had paid attention, I'da been ready.

CHAPTER NINE

# *Peace Be Still*

When Jim, Mae, Miss Brown, and I walked into Calvary that morning, you'd've thought we came in with no underwear on. Folks turned all the way 'round in they seats and got to whispering loud enough for a deaf man to hear. Men went into coughing fits on account of they dealings with Mae. Women were saying things like *How she think she can just come up in here? Who she think she is?* Then, I heard Lucy, who'd been Mae's running partner back in the day, talk about the devil being busy. Now, Lucy had gotten into the church years ago, but not before she had done her own share of dirt. It's a crying shame how folks think that getting old is supposed to erase all they did but let them remember what everybody else used to do. I cut her a look and wished that she could hear my thoughts too. I guess my look was good enough, 'cause she turn her face back 'round toward the front. We went up to the same seat we been sitting in when I feel Mae pulling back.

"I'll just sit back here," she say.

"No, Mae," I told her. "You our guest, so you'll sit with us."

Miss Brown was grinning like she really was crazy. I guess she just happy to be out the house. The so-called "saved folks" kept whispering right up 'til the preachers walked in along with the choir. When they came in, we heard more of the same from a different group. Reverend DuBois looked at us and nodded though. That made me glad. He was one of the few men not ashamed to see Mae in church. Matter fact, he looked downright happy. A couple men coughed so hard, they had to go outside. One woman was so mad she just got up and left. Believe me when I tell you, with the exception of old man Wilson, we had our whole pew to ourselves. Mr. Wilson looked too happy to be next to Miss Brown. Me and Jim could hear how he had always liked her. We tried to shut out all the noise of them folks. It's funny how listening can be louder than talking.

Anyway, Reverend DuBois taught on forgiveness, and I knew that he hadn't intended that for his text. He talked about how forgiving somebody else wouldn't get them off the hook, but it sure would let you off. Most folks in there thought he was talking to them and telling them that they should forgive Mae. I knew though, he was really speaking to Mae's heart and all the hurt she had to endure. He said that our lives get clouded with hatred for all that's been done to us, and we can't receive none of the things that are for us. Mae cried, and so did Miss Brown.

After church, a few of them self-righteous folks had the nerve to tell Mae that they forgave her. They did it right there in front of everybody like she was some kind of voodoo doll that needed to be stuck for they own pain. To her credit, Mae ain't say a word, but I could hear what she was thinking.

"And I forgive you for trying to have me in the same way your husband did," she say in her mind for one woman.

"You forgive me?" she thought to another. "Your man was so bad you ought to thank me, one, for taking him off your hands and two, for teaching him a few things."

I was trying to hold back my laugh when I caught Jim's eyes and saw he was laughing too. When we got out to the car, Mr. Wilson said he'd like to escort Miss Brown back home. He winked at Jim, and Jim smiled back. Just as we were about to drive off, Irma Allen, Mr. Stan's wife, came running up alongside the car door.

"Louella, Louella," she yell.

I rolled down the window to talk, and I see tears in her eyes.

"Thank you," she managed to say.

I can see all that she thanking me for, and I just smile.

"You just beginning," I tell her. "But you gotta help him keep things on the right track."

She grabbed my hand and tell me thank you again.

"You alright by me, Louella Johnson," she say. She look in the back, and say, "Hey, Mae, I heard somebody say you came by trying to volunteer at the day care."

Mae looked kinda bashful all of a sudden and say, "Yes, but I realized I couldn't do it after all."

"You don't fool me, Mae. You took one look at them kids and didn't want no part of it, did you?" she winked at Mae, and they both laughed.

"Girl, me and Stanuel got all kinds of work we need help with, if you don't mind getting dirty."

Mae was about to ask what kind of work when she decided it didn't matter. She was gonna have something she could put her hands to, and in doing so, she was going to get her peace.

CHAPTER TEN

# Peace and Blessings

Now, I am not one for all them new gadgets, but my children insisted on getting me an answering machine and one of the caller ID boxes. I think them boxes are for crazy folks who need to go on *Oprah* when Dr. Phil's there. Anybody who like to trace down where all they phone calls are coming from is a little on the paranoid side. But my son convinced me of it, since he calls from all over the place and sometimes forgets to leave the phone number where he's staying. Anyway, when we got back from church, we had fifteen calls on our machine. Folks all took they turn at telling us that we was low to bring somebody like Mae into the Lord's house. One woman said God was not pleased and that he would see to it that we were properly taken care of. I know her voice even without looking at the number. It was Mae's old running buddy, Lucy. I wondered how she ever had the gall to use the word "proper," since wasn't nothing about her that way. The calls were all saying the same thing, and I was getting right tired of hearing it. I was about to hang up when I heard my son, Neal, or Naim as he called himself, on the machine.

"Hello, Queen Mother, this is your son, Naim. I have finished the writing of my dissertation and have some time before my defense. I'll be home in a few days to rest in the comfort of my first teachers. I surely hope my father has not taken it upon himself to alter my living quarters in any way. Peace and blessings," he say before the machine started yelling at us again.

Jim walked into the room just long enough to hear the part about not altering the living quarters. He laughed one of his real good, belly laughs.

"Louella," Jim say, "your child is crazy."

The children always belonged to me when they did something ridiculous. But still I could tell that Jim was glad to be able to see one of his children. Jim Johnson was the kind of man who grew into himself as his children did. He was at the birth of every one of them kids, and he did more that his share of raising them. I hardly ever had to get up out of bed in the night when they was still babies, screaming for my milk. Jim would walk over to our makeshift bassinet, which was really a dresser drawer, and hold that child in his arms 'til the baby calmed down. He said his mama told him that it was not good for a baby to be too upset when they was eating. She told him it was bad for the mama and the baby. By the time that child was nursing, they was as calm as the storm that Jesus spoke to. When they was still growing up, Jim took the boys and the girls fishing, taught them all how to build things, and showed them how to read the stars. He said his daddy had taught him, and that it was important to know. I didn't understand nothing 'bout no stars, and still don't. But if Jim say it's real important, then I know that it is. Now my Jim is a godly man, but the truth of the matter is he goes to church only 'cause I want him to. The Johnson family were a strange bunch. They held secret meetings that only their family members attended. My mama say they were doing things like that for as long as anybody knew them. There were tales about the Johnsons that went back as far as anybody can remember. That's one reason why everybody respect him so, 'cause they can't figure them out. Jim use to wake up at night and go out and look up at the stars. He never took me though. I figured it was for him and his children, so I never questioned it. It didn't seem like I should, for some reason.

There I go again. I got way over there into Jim's family's strangeness when I was trying to tell you 'bout the way he is with his children. Now Neal, or Naim, as he say his name really is, is crazy as they come. But seem to me that he give Jim the most joy. They can go off for hours, and I declare I don't know what the two of them can be talking 'bout. The boy is gonna be a doctor of philosophy, which from what he say, is thinking about thinking. Now when he first tell me that he gonna do this, I ask him why he don't just become a regular doctor. They make good money, and they help folks. He was always one to try to fix things. If his brother or sisters got into arguments, Neal would try to make peace. He was always bringing some half-dead animal 'round back to make it better. If he couldn't, well he'd give it a funeral, and he and the rest of them kids would act out all the parts. Back then, I thought he was gonna be a preacher on account of that was the part he always played. When Neal was real young, he was filled with questions about how things work and what does this word mean, where do the sky come from, and if God made the sky, who in the world could've made God. Neal didn't really like church though. That's when I knew the preacher business was out. He went to church for the same reason his daddy did, 'cause I wanted him to, but unlike the other kids, he never fussed about it.

I was glad that Neal was coming home. When you use to a lot of commotion, it takes a while to adjust to not having it. I guess that put an end to me and Jim's kitchen and living room business, which reminded me of all that I was gonna have to do to get a place ready for that boy to sleep. I had no intentions of moving Mae out of Neal's "living quarters," as he called them, not even to the back bedroom. She was comfortable and happy in that crazy mess that boy had created, so I wasn't gonna take that away from her too.

We had a nice, peaceful Sunday dinner. Mae even offered to do the dishes. I let her 'til she broke two of my good plates. That's when I told Jim to take over. When we were done, Mae said she was tired, and Jim went to work on something in the garage. I went to cleaning the back bedroom, never worrying about the fact that Mae was just above Jim's head. Shucks, the way things were between me and Jim, there would never be anything that we didn't know about or understand. I never really was afraid before now, but evil got a way of creeping in just the same. Old folks used to say don't worry, but you got to wonder. I did wonder from time to time, 'cause so many folks were looking at my Jim right after we got married. Funny how some old things can sit in a store window for a long time with not a soul wanting anything like it. Seem like Jim was like that. Wasn't a whole lot of girls paying no attention to Jim 'til he start to pay attention to me. Then all of a sudden, they batting they eyes and switching by him like he new in town. Jim didn't look to his left or his right. He got his mind fixed on me and wouldn't nothing change it. Part of the reason nobody was interested before Jim start to look at me was because of how strange his family was. But after he keep company with me, none of that mattered to any one of them. There were a few times Jim slipped up. But he told me about it and worked to make things right. I told my mama 'bout those times, but all she said was, "Baby, love is patient." Back then, I just cried and cried, but now with all that's gone on between us, I know just what she means. I was thinking on all of that as I was cleaning out that back room. It hadn't been used since Christmas a year ago when all the kids came home. I love that time of year. All the kids and they kids pile into my little house and laugh and talk into the wee hours of the morning. Seem like the room still smell like the orange and clove balls that the babies made for me. I knew wasn't none in there 'cause I have given that room a good cleaning every month or so. Just as I finished the last bit of sweeping, I heard knocking at our front door.

"Mama," I heard Neal's deep voice say, "let me in, Mama, unless you and Daddy doing something that I don't want to see."

I can't explain all the joy that rushed into my heart and head at that point. I'll tell you this though, I felt like I did back when Jim first started courting me, and I'd get all flushed whenever he came around. Don't go thinking I had no funny feelings for my child. That's not what I'm saying. But ask any mother whose baby done grown up to look like and act like his father if the sight of him don't make them feel young again. That's how I feel about Neal, all young and ready to be falling into love.

"I'm coming," I yelled back.

When I opened the door and saw my beautiful boy, I almost cried.

"Peace and blessings, Naim," I said to him instead.

He smiled that same pulled-back smile that his daddy does when he's trying hard not to laugh at me.

"Peace and blessings, Mother. Peace and many many blessings."

# CHAPTER ELEVEN

## Lost Love

Naim and I stood in the doorway, hugging each other for so long that it took me a minute to see that he was not alone. When I let go of him, I punched his arm playfully.

"You said you wouldn't be home for a few days."

"I wanted to surprise you and Daddy, and well, you can never do that to old people. You all have a way of sensing stuff. I guess you can smell us coming, huh?"

It was then that I noticed the man that was standing behind my boy.

"Watch your mouth, boy. You outnumbered by old folks," he said.

Standing there on my porch under the glow of the yellow

bulb was a man that looked more like Jim's people than Jim did. He looked so much like Jim and the way Jim's daddy did when we were young 'til I got a bit confused. Neal looking like my man and this man looking like his daddy, I felt like time had gone backward, and I was caught up in it.

"Mama," Neal say, "this is John, a friend and fellow colleague. We met in the library at the university."

My mind was telling me that Neal was saying something about "Are you going to invite us in?" but I couldn't think, speak, or move. It wasn't until Jim came up behind us and yelled, "John Johnson, we thought you was dead," that I felt myself come to.

Life got a way of coming back 'round to where it started. In all the years we had been together, Jim never told me about no brother that he didn't really know. It became clear that Mr. Johnson didn't bother to tell Neal either. Jim and John hugged and cried for so long that me and Neal wondered when we would be let in on the truth. That's when I really came back to myself and realized that if I'd shut up with all my thinking, I'd be able to hear them thinking.

"Mama said we had to find you," Jim was saying to John's head. "She told us that you were the link to ourselves. I used to think of you as the missing link."

Jim and his brother were laughing together, but all Neal and I could see was smiles and tears.

"This is my wife, Louella Johnson," Jim said out loud.

Jim's brother stared at me hard, and then he was all up in my head.

"You hear too, don't you?" he said, more like he was telling me than asking me.

"You are as beautiful a person as you are in your son's heart." Now truth ain't never been nothing to shame, so I'ma tell it. I was scared of this man. I had only secretly come into this gift, but I know that he had been this way from the time of his birth. I done already told you that my grandmother and some other relatives were gifted, but it didn't feel nothing like what this man had. As soon as I thought it, I wished I hadn't. It was like trying to get your words back after you done gone and told somebody something you shouldn't. Only it's harder with thinking, and even worse with Jim's brother. I instantly could feel that John's hearing was harnessed like a mule to a plow. It had been disciplined and made to go where it was needed. John smiled at me and nodded.

"Lord," I say out loud. "I don't know if I'm gonna be able to bear all of this."

"Oh, Mama, you have always acted as if being and living are two different things. I too am shocked to find that this is my natural uncle, but from the moment we met, I felt connected in a way that went beyond the known."

Neal talked like a book that folks buy just to say that

they have it. Books that you start to read but have a hard time getting to the story on account of all them words.

"Son," Jim say, "you have no idea what your mama's talking about, but when you do find out, you gonna want to give all them degrees back and try to know what she know."

Now I had to laugh 'cause in his own way, Jim was saying that I was smarter than Neal, which made my heart feel what I call border-proud. That's being so proud that it's on the border of being too prideful. I winked at Jim, and then I went into my kitchen where I am always at peace. I musta got caught up in my thinking, 'cause by the time I come back to myself, I had cooked and re-heated a whole mess of food. Just when I laid it all out on the dining table, Mae came down to offer her help. She musta heard all the voices 'cause she had dressed herself up like the old Mae. Before I started thinking on old habits and how hard they die, I remembered that Mae didn't bring much with her so she was doing the best she could with what she had.

"You can help by eating," I tell Mae.

"Girl, we got us some company."

When Neal, Jim, and John came into our dining room, I thought Mae was gonna pass out like the women did in the books I used to read when I was a girl. I have always loved to read. There wasn't much to choose from then, so I couldn't be much too choosy. My teacher used to tell me that I was the best reader she had. I can't remember not wanting to read. But that's one of the benefits of having a big family. The younger children learn what the older ones know, then they learn on top of that. I was next to the youngest so I got to know plenty. I read whatever my brothers and sisters read before I even started school. I remember overhearing the teacher tell my mama that I should go to college. She said if I didn't, my life would be a waste, and I'd end up as my mama did with a mess of children and nothing to show for it. That's when my mama told her that she was the one trying to raise other people's kids since she ain't had none of her own.

Then my mama say, "Miss Teacher, if my life is such a waste, why are you standing here praising my child?"

That answer sent her right on out of our little town. She said that she couldn't be bothered with trying to elevate the thinking of such backward people. I sometimes wonder where she went and how she lived out her life. I hope she found one, 'cause I sure did. Still, I thank her for making me feel special. It don't matter no more that she couldn't see the special in my mama though. I'm sure glad I did, 'cause having a mess of babies and a home full of love beat any other life she thought I needed.

Well, I need to tell you 'bout the night Jim's brother came home, but I keep wandering off into old memories. I do that sometimes when the new day is too bright. That's how I know change is hard for folks. It ain't like they don't know they need to change or that they can. What keep most folks in the same place year after year is that they know where they are, no matter how bad or simple or low it may be. Knowing how to get around in mess always seems easier than stepping out of it, 'cause when you step out, you don't know where you are no more. Anyway, I said all of that to say that Jim's brother brought a lot of change into our lives and in our little town. But there I go again, getting to the end before I can tell you the beginning. Let me back up, so I can bring you through.

# CHAPTER TWELVE

# Life's Pleasures

$\mathcal{J}$im's brother came into my dining room that was smelling like heaven would, if they had food up there. But I know they don't on account of we shall be like Him, and our bodies ain't gonna have no time for earthly things. Anyway, my food was smelling good. John took one look at the table and started to rubbing his head. I knew he was trying to figure out what he was gonna eat first. As soon as he heard my thought, or better yet even sooner, as I have come to know, John said, "You got me right, Louella Johnson. I want to sit right on top of this table and welcome myself back home."

Just as he was saying this, Mae walked in with the last plate. It was as full of biscuits as Mae's mouth was.

"Girl, I don't know what you put in these, but Lord knows they good through and through."

"And so are you," John say to Mae.

He stared at her long and hard, and I could hear and somehow see him talking to Mae's mind and opening the door so the thoughts could rush in. Now, what I'm gonna say next will sound like a line from one of them old books my teacher used to let me read. Things happened so quickly that I can't even remember the beginning. Well, that ain't quite the way the line go, but it's something like that.

John took Mae by the hand, introduced himself as Jim's brother who he hadn't seen in more than fifty years, and told her to sit next to him.

"You have less time here than my family will have with me, and I'm going to spend every minute of it loving you."

Now, I wish I can tell you that things don't happen that quickly in real life, but sometimes they do. Folks who don't believe in love at first sight don't understand the ways of our ancestors. First sight ain't really first. I know this on account of what my grandmother and my mother always told me: "Ain't nothing new under the sun."

"If it ain't new, it ain't first," they would say. "Just live long enough and you'll see life roll its way back to the beginning and move on again."

Now, I don't believe in what Neal calls "reincarnation." He says it's the coming back of the self over and over until we right our wrongs and become one with God. But I done already told you my son is real smart, so smart he crazy. When I meet my Jesus, ain't gonna be no need to come back and fix nothing. Jesus did that on the cross. We just gotta live in the life we got. Anyway, I don't see life that way, but I do think that what we live and don't live is passed on to our children and the children we come in contact with. I told Neal that a while back. Reincarnation is like reinvention. It's only a new thing once, then it's a renovation. Well, that just got his mind to think so hard that he ain't come down from his ole park room for a few days. When he did, he tell me that I am a wise woman, then he say he had to go back to school to pursue the truth of his existence. Well, I told you he was crazy, didn't I? Anyway, Mae and John didn't reinvent love. They renovated themselves to be ready to receive it. They love wasn't physical though. It was the love that Pastor DuBois call the highest form, *"agape."* It was far reaching; a love that had crossed time lines and generations to find itself again, even if it was just for a short while. Besides, doing right for a little while had a much longer impact than living wrong for a long time. It's usually the folks who are watching the doing who decided that the change ain't real or long enough.

Whoo, I'm getting long-winded, even for me. I'm even starting to sound like my crazy chile do with all his thinking about thinking. But like they say, apple don't fall far from the tree. I use to wonder why they said apple instead of an orange or better yet a pineapple, 'cause you know that really don't roll too far. Maybe it was a pineapple and somebody shortened it. Well now I know I'm proving my own point. I'm proving it so well that I'm starting to think that maybe it was me that made my boy as crazy as he is. Don't worry, I'm gonna get to what happened. John and Mae sat next to each other and ate like they ain't never ate before. Me and Jim always get hungry after we do the do. Seem like they got hungry instead of doing it. Jim watch me watching them and start to laughing.

"Get outta folks' business, Louella Johnson," he say.

Neal was too busy eating food that could kill him to see all that was going on. With all them smarts, he didn't notice the differences in our little house. It was not until after he was finished eating and was trying to get out of cleaning up that he found out his room wasn't his no more. I guess he was too tired and too full to argue. But what he didn't get to say that night found its way into his head and out of his mouth the next morning. That's when I knew for sure that you can spoil kids even when you ain't got much to give them.

Neal came out to breakfast as soon as he smell the butter hit the skillet.

"Something smells wonderful, Mother."

He kissed me on my cheek and sat in the spot he claimed when he was still a willful boy.

"Ain't nothing really cooking but butter, but you always did love the smell of something that came from an animal, even if you do refuse to eat it now. Don't worry," I told him. "I'm gonna make you some nice grits without milk, butter, or sugar. I do remember you telling me that sugar was the reason for slavery. God knows I don't want to make you think that all Black folks amount to is some sugar."

"Well, Mother," Neal say real slow, "since my last visit, I've had an epiphany concerning many things. One such revelation pertains to my eating rituals."

"Boy, stop your nonsense and talk with the tongue God gave you. If you want sugar or butter in your grits, just ask for it. You can't cuss a French man in English."

Neal, or Naim, or whoever he is since he had his 'piffany, rocked back in his chair like he done seen all the men in our family do, and said, "Touché, Mother, touché."

I guess he got the point, but missed the blade. But that's alright. He my child and as much like me as he is like Jim, and I like them two just fine. Anyway, while I was cooking, he decide to tell me that he was disturbed by Miss Mae taking over his living quarters. He ask how long she gonna be there and when can he move back to his room. I left him to his thoughts long enough to remember how to show respect. Good thing too, 'cause it was right around that time that Jim came in. Now, I know most folks don't believe in what they call corporal punishment. We didn't know nothing 'bout corporals or sergeants or anything else that have something to do with war, but when you raising kids in love and truth, sometimes you just got to let them know which way to walk. I have been known to "go off" as my children like to say, but it was always Jim who showed them the light. "Go get my belt so I can show you the light," he used to tell them. It don't matter how grown them kids get, Jim still tell them that he will show them the light, even though he stopped when they reach sixteen. I do believe though that they think he'll do it even now. Well, when Jim walk in and hear my thoughts trying to be calm on account of our son being mannish, he give Neal "the look."

"Boy, do you want to have to tell all them high-and-mighty folks up North how your daddy had to show you the light?"

Neal tried to laugh it off, but Jim wasn't playing. And Neal could just about taste Jim's temper.

"I see the walls still have ears. We never could get away with anything around here. What was the phrase you were so fond of, Mother?" He raised his voice and put his hand on his hips and tried his best to look and sound like me. "You children know we can hear a rat pee on cotton."

"Boy, go get my belt," Jim say. He had stood over Neal's seat and looked down at him like he meant business.

He tried to laugh, and Jim looked at him like he was really crazy. Now, I knew that in his head, Jim was laughing. But he still didn't show it, and I had to fight hard to do the same. Well, I lost the battle, but won the war. I laughed so hard that Jim did too, and Neal, bless his heart, found a way to pick his face up off the floor. He also learned a thing or two about how his daddy done got better with his age, but respect and good behavior don't have no limit. They just are and should be.

After we got tired from laughing, I told Neal that he wasn't getting what he referred to as his room no time soon.

"As a matter of fact," I say, "it don't really become your room 'til me and your daddy go on to meet our maker."

"That's right," Jim tells him. "From the way me and your mama been feeling, that's gonna be a real long time."

Jim put his arms around me and look at Neal like he was daring him to say something.

"If you want to know what I know, son, you would spend a little less time in them books and find some time for love. When you do that, maybe I'll tell you the secret to your mama's good cooking."

Jim pinched me on the behind right there in front of my son. This was something he never did. True, they always know we really loved each other, but we never got real showy in front of our kids. I guess we were just trying to respect the order of life. Neal turned his head and tried hard not to notice what was going on, but me and Jim both heard him thinking, "What in the name of Amenhotep is going on with these two?"

We didn't know much about what he was thinking, 'cept I remembered something I saw on the Discovery Channel 'bout how Amenhotep was a great math man who laid out the plans for the pyramids. I guess he was saying, "What in creation are my parents doing?"

Jim caught my thinking drift and said, to my head, "Leave him alone, Louella. At least he ain't say, 'What in the Sam hell?'"

We laughed some more and heard Jim's brother John laughing on his way into the kitchen. He had stayed in the kids' room that we had made up for him. I think he would've liked to have stayed with Mae, but I heard her tell him that she wanted to make love to him in her dreams. Now, I guess she done lost more habits than I know. Sometimes it's better to get rid of the ones that's destroying your temple than it is to mess with the little bugs that's just trying to stay warm. When Mae came in the kitchen, a few bugs came with her, like her, asking for coffee and biscuits but not getting up to help none. I didn't even bother to swat at that gnat. I just thanked God that she was finally living for love.

Well, Mae and John ate like they didn't get no food the night before. When they were done, John and Neal did the dishes, while me, Jim, and Mae got ready for the day. Now I gotta move back before I go forward. Jim decided that he would take a vacation from work. Believe me when I tell you the only real vacation time he ever took was for the birth of our children. Back then Jim would take off a whole two weeks for each and every one of them. It's not like we didn't want to go no place, it was just that we didn't have a whole lot of money to go with all of our needs. Educating our children so they could go all over the world was more important than going someplace and leaving them dumb. We saved in ways that we didn't have to feel. Jim always reckoned that if we ain't have something, we wouldn't get no taste for it. Most of the things folks call luxuries never even made their way into our house. We'd drive a car 'til it couldn't drive no more, and we wore clothes and shoes the same way. With the exception of my wedding ring, which is just a silver band that all the women in his family wear, I have no jewelry. Jim used to say that no diamond could compete

with my eyes. At first I thought he was being cheap and decided that I could do way worse than having a man who was thrifty. It was not until one of my brothers came to town with what must have been his fifth wife. Now, my brother has done real well in the money department, but when it comes to women, he don't do too good. He done grown into being a real, decent man, but his wife picker is broke. This wife, Anna Marie Cooper-Givens, on account she said she wanted to have all of her names, is a doozie. Now, I understand all the name things that happen with marriage, I just don't know why folks get uppity if they decide to have six names and get mad if you only remember four. My daughter, Otha, the one I told you about before is all business, she kept her name. She say that getting married at thirty-five and changing your name the next day is like moving a thirty-five-year-old business but not leaving a forwarding address.

Well, my brother's wife say different. She say if you love a man enough to marry him, you ought to love him enough to take his name. I married Jim long before these kind of conversations were thought of. Back then it wasn't even a question. You got married, you took your husband's name. Most women were so proud to be married, they even lost they first name. I think Anna Marie Cooper-Givens need to have all her names all the time on account of she wasn't sure who she was.

I was talking 'bout how I used to think that Jim was

just being cheap when he tell me that I don't need no diamonds to race against my eyes. Well, I knew he was being true when my brother's wife, I call her that 'cause she act like she ain't related to nobody in his family but him, came to town in their new car, wearing her new big, one-year anniversary diamond. Now, I ain't had no jealousy about nothing much since I know that if you do whatever somebody did to get what they done got, you can get it too. I have always been annoyed by people who are envious of what somebody else got. When Mr. Wilson from down the street got a brand new Lincoln Town Car that he paid for in cash, thank you very much, folks got all mad and said stuff like, "Who that ole fool think he is with that nice car? Ain't nobody gonna want him just 'cause he got a new car." Now, when you listen to folks talk bad about somebody else, you can hear what they saying about theyself. What I heard them saying was they try to get stuff to impress somebody not 'cause it's what they like. Ain't no need to be jealous of Mr. Wilson. All you gotta do is work hard like he did, put in for all the overtime like he did, save your money like he did, and buy whatever car you want. Folks who get jealous ain't really mad 'cause you got what they want. They mad 'cause you were willing to do what they wasn't, and that's work for it. I told you all that 'bout Mr. Wilson's car and all to let you know that what I'm 'bout to say about my brother's wife and her big anniversary diamond ain't got nothing to do with jealousy. And I pray that it ain't about pride. Anyway, she came in flapping her hand all over the place like there was a bee 'round her head. I ask her if she okay, and she say, "Yes, Lou." She call me Lou, even after I told her my name Louella, on account of Lou's Jim's special name.

"Yes, Lou, I'm just trying to work out the kink in my wrist. Maybe it's this new ring. I must ask the jeweler if he sized it properly."

I had already seen the thing on her hand and didn't feel like having small talk about a big ring. She put her hand so close to my face that if I didn't say something, she'd a made my brother trade it for something bigger.

"Wow," I say, like I was in a commercial. "That sure is a big ring. You must be doing something mighty good for Baby Brother to go out and get a ring like that."

Now, my brother's name is Ray, but we ain't ever call him nothing but Baby Brother. Can you believe that boy called me before his wife came to meet us for the first time (since we weren't invited to the wedding) and had the nerve to tell me to call him Ray in front of his new wife? I called all my brothers and sisters 'cause I believe a good laugh should be shared with family. They all laughed 'til they cried. I must have Baby Brothered him to death. I called his name like folks who think they know how to pray do when they talk to God, "Father God this and Father God that."

I was saying things like, "Baby Brother, how you feeling, Baby Brother? It's sure good to see you, Baby Brother, 'cause you the baby brother." I was so bad that he was afraid to talk on account that he knew I was gonna find a way to make Baby Brother the subject, verb, and pronoun. Lord, he was mad, but ain't none of us Givens can stay mad at another one for too long. After a while, when I got tired of calling him Baby Brother, I took to calling Anna Marie Cooper-Givens Baby Sis. Ray got to laughing harder than I was, and we started snorting and hiccuping like we used to do when we were kids. Baby Sis had all she could take and told us that she would be checking into a hotel. Baby Brother kept on laughing but managed to tell me that he loved me and thanked me for my truth.

"My wife will need a little time to get used to us," he said.

"That's fine," I tell him. "But when Paul went to Rome, he didn't really do as the Romans did."

My brother knew just what I was talking about. Our grandmother would tell all of her grand- and great-grandkids, "When you leave this house, remember that you are a Givens, and anything you do will leave a mark or stain on everyone in this family."

She'd say, "Don't do what you see other folks do. Do what you know is right."

One of my crazy sisters got to thinking that Grandma

Sadie couldn't hear her thoughts and said, "Well, when in Rome do as the Romans do." She said this in her head, where my grandma could hear not just her thoughts but her intentions as well. That's when my grandma sat her down and read to her about how Paul went all kinds of places winning souls for Christ. Not once did he act like the folks he was sent to help. My brother knew that I was telling him to help his wife learn to be free, but don't get in the cage with her when you go to let her out. He hugged me and thanked me for the short visit and told me he would be back soon. I guess his dictionary say that "soon" is a year, 'cause that's when they came back. Anyway, I was telling you how my brother's wife don't like to hear him called Baby Brother, and how she was flapping that new ring of hers.

"I didn't have to do anything for Raymond. He loves me the way I am. This ring is an expression of his love."

She looked down at that plain silver band on my finger and then held up her hand to get another look at her own. Then she was crazy enough to look over at Jim, who never said much, but said even less to her.

"Mrs. Anna Marie Cooper-Givens," Jim say without blinking, "I don't have to put nothing on my wife's hand to show her that I love her. You see how pretty her eyes are? That's 'cause I put my love inside her, and it shines through them big, brown eyes."

The last thing he said was, "The eyes are the window to the soul, not a store-bought diamond."

Well, you know we ain't seen them since, though my brother calls from work at least every two weeks.

Look at me, I got way over here on Ray's wife's diamond, trying to tell you about how we ain't use our money on nothing folks call luxury. But like I always say, life got a way of working back around to the past. When Jim's brother and our son came home the night before, Jim decided that it was time to go into the time he got saved up.

"Folks can't ever enjoy the real good stuff if they use up they life on something useless," Jim say.

He called his job and told them that he would be taking a three-week vacation. They needed him bad, but wasn't nothing they could do. Jim had saved up enough vacation that he was due about a year of paid leave. We ain't go nowhere. Folks sure did get to wondering and whispering on what it was we was up to. Having Mae in our house all day long with some strange man didn't help things none.

"Good grits and gravy." It done took me a whole fifteen minutes to explain why Jim was still home in the middle of the morning. I hope I ain't sounding like one of them books Neal's always saying is important. I think I go on and on like that 'cause Janet, one of my old friends from high school, used to say, "Louella, life is all in the corners."

She was and still is what my grandmother would call "a beautiful soul." She say things that made her sound like she was not of this world. We'd be walking home from school or combing each other's hair, something girls did back then to have fun, and she'd say things that cut to the quick of your understanding. I was scratching her scalp on our porch one day when Janet say, "Life is all in the corners. People try to live on the surface of life, but you got to get down in the corners to find the joy." I guess my scratching brought up more than her dandruff, 'cause I got to thinking on that from the day she said it to this one.

Janet don't live down here no more, but I still hear from her. We grew apart only in geography. She went off to school and learned how to find and look at all kinds of things that's hidden in the corners. She's what's called an archaeologist, and I'm proud to know someone who took they good life-sense and watered the book-sense. She writes to me a lot and sometimes she'll call from all over the world. She says she had always loved the way I talk and talk all over things 'cause I show you really where I'm coming from with what I'm saying. One time Janet told me she would never marry until she could find a man like me. She ain't that way or nothing. She just saying she wants somebody she can talk to like we do. Well,

I'm glad somebody appreciate my rambling, 'cause it done get me in lots of trouble. That's what happen on the second week of me and Jim's stay-at-home vacation. I got to saying more than I needed to and almost got us all into a mess of trouble. Still, wasn't no need for nobody to get upset, 'cause it was also my talking that got us out.

# CHAPTER THIRTEEN

## Living the Truth

$F$olks ain't take too well to not knowing what was going on in my house. I never been able to make sense of why folks think they need to know everything about somebody else. My Aunt T, who came to me that night with my mama and grandmother Sadie, used to say what I eat won't make you poop. Aunt T was never wrapped too tight, but she was always easy to love. That's 'cause she was so to the point that you either had to laugh or get mad. We chose to laugh, 'cause anger does not achieve the righteousness of God. Anyway, folks started coming over to see what we was doing and who this new woman in our house was. They were also wondering why Neal was home and if he had become a doctor yet. Practically everybody in town thought he was gonna be a medical doctor, and I guess he got tired of telling them any different. Now, my son done got book crazy, but he still a Johnson, through and through. One day Sister Harper ask him what she should be taking for her arthritis 'cause what her doctor is giving her ain't working. Neal tell her to bathe in Epsom salts and sleep with pennies on her knees. She thanked him and said how she always knew he was gonna be somebody. When she left, Jim popped Neal upside his head and asked him if he had lost the little bit of mind that was left. Neal got to talking all big again, saying something 'bout if a situation is defined as real, it's real in its outcome. The look on my face musta been saying, "Boy, what are you talking about?" 'cause he took it on himself to explain.

"Sister Harper believes that I am a doctor. It does not matter to her what kind of doctor I am going to be. She believes me to be a medical doctor; therefore, all ideas coming from me and their outcome are determined from her perspective of me as a doctor."

Neal's brother, Nathan, who was also home visiting, looked at Neal and said, "Toby, talk English. You in America. You no more Africa Guinea, man."

I knew he was quoting a line from *Roots* because when they got together, the kids would talk in lines from all the movies they watched when they were coming up. Even Neal had to laugh at himself.

"All I'm saying is if she believes I'm a doctor, she will believe in my ability to heal her."

"Well, son," Jim told him, "looks like you were paying attention in Sunday school."

Neal still hadn't seen the connection, but we love him just the same. Anyway, folks was coming over to see what we were up to and as soon as they came into our home, they brought all they joy and sadness with them. Jim said with all this thinking we was able to do, we needed to be put in quarantine. First one to find their way to our house was Mr. Broadnax. That was the man who Jim heard thinking about wanting his lips on Jim's privates.

He knocked on the door, and Mae let him in. We were sitting in the kitchen having a cup of tea, enjoying each other's silence. Mae showed Mr. Broadnax into our kitchen. He looked so embarrassed that I started to feel shame too. Now, Jim is what you might call a manly man, but that has never stopped him from caring about how somebody else feel.

"Afternoon, Henry."

"Afternoon, Jim," he said, like nothing had ever happened to make Jim slam the phone down in his ear. I excused myself 'cause I was starting to feel like I was the one who had exposed myself to Jim, plus I know this man didn't want to talk his business in front of the wife of the man he was lusting for. Anyway, you and I both know that I didn't need to be in that room to hear what was going on.

Jim told Mr. Broadnax to have a seat and offered him some coffee. I heard Jim saying in his head that Broadnax probably liked it with a lot of sugar since he was so sweet. Then he asked for forgiveness. After he did that he said, "Louella Johnson, get out of my head." I laughed and told his mind to hush and listen to what the man had to say.

"I'm sorry for any trouble I caused you, Jim. I really am. I guess I got beside myself and started talking out loud. I never meant for you to hear what I been thinking all these years."

Jim raced over the work shifts and lunch breaks he had shared with Broadnax. He went all the way back to how Broadnax first took him under his wing when he started at the plant. Then Jim told Broadnax how he was glad to see that he was the first one to congratulate him when he was made supervisor over the same man who trained him.

"You deserved it," Broadnax say. "Nobody works harder or better than you do."

Jim was thinking on how he was glad he couldn't hear thoughts back then, since he was too young to know how to forgive something like this. That's when I heard his brother, John, telling Jim's head that gifts and lessons can only be appreciated when they're opened at the proper time. Now, you know I don't lie, and I don't scare that easy, but what Jim's brother was doing was downright spooky. John had taken Mae out fishing. When he asked her to get ready to go, she commence to crying. I was about to ask her what was wrong, when I remember to shut up and listen. She was thinking on how in all her life, no man had ever taken her out in the daylight. I wanted to cry with her, but I know that she was on her way back through. Sometimes it seem like the healing process hurts worse than the sickness, but once you get through, you better than before. "Better to take bitter medicine than to die of consumption," my grandmama say.

Well, I'm listening to John talk in Jim's head and at the same time I'm hearing Jim all up in Broadnax's thoughts. I guess I felt like Peter walking out on that water with Jesus. He was fine 'til he saw what he was able to do. Then all a sudden, the thing he had already done seemed impossible for him to do. Well, as if I hadn't been through enough in my head, I heard John tell me nothing is impossible to him that believe. Instead of getting all crazy, I decide to walk boldly in purpose.

I can see them sitting over by the lake fishing. I tell you it's a powerful thing to be able to talk to folks when they miles away.

"How y'all doing out there?" I ask John. "You catch anything?" I ask.

"Nope," his thought spoke back. "I got all I need sitting next to me."

"Good," I tell him back. "Then I won't have to cut and gut. Y'all have a nice time."

"We will," he thought back. "By the way, Louella, this gift can turn on and off. Remind me to teach you how. And I'll teach you how to shut others out."

His thoughts came to me right before my next thought came to my conscious. I had just been wondering why I couldn't hear him lately when I had heard him so clearly before.

" 'Cause I don't want you to. Don't worry, Louella Johnson," he say. "I will not leave you without telling you all that you need to know."

I didn't hear him again until he was on his way back to our house.

Mr. Broadnax had a real good talk with Jim and wasn't hiding himself from him no more. And he had no idea that it would be impossible if he tried. Broadnax told Jim how he had always been afraid of someone discovering who he really was.

"I was afraid I would lose my job if anybody knew," he say.

"Why you telling me all this?" Jim asked.

" 'Cause I needed someone to know who I am. I guess that my slipup the other day was my mind telling me that I could trust you to know. I'm gonna be moving away," Broadnax said. "And I have always loved you, Jim. I guess I needed to fantasize about something since I couldn't do or go nowhere for real. Anyway, I can't live this way no more. All my life I tried to change, but this is who I am. Not ever being who you are can kill you. I done had more affairs than Monica Lew"—he stumbled over the name, and then said—"you know who I mean, the one that kept that nasty dress. Anyhow, I have affairs in my mind 'cause I can't have them in real life. If anybody knew how I was feeling 'bout them, they'd bring back public lynching." I knew that Broadnax said *"public lynching"* 'cause we all suspected that they still went on in private.

"I am what I am, Jim, but I'm living a lie. Hard thing is, I don't even know what it would really feel like to be with anybody."

Jim started blinking, and even if I couldn't hear, I would've known that he was thinking real hard.

"How you know you like men if you ain't never been with them? And how you know you don't like women if you ain't ever love one?"

Mr. Broadnax had surely asked himself the same thing over and over, 'cause he was ready with his answer.

"I know because I know. It's time for me to find out for sure."

Jim was thinking, "Wear a rubber, man. You old and you stupid." But all he said was "Be careful. Anything that's new can be dangerous when you don't know what it's for."

Now, Jim ain't one to judge, so I know he wasn't trying to be like Mr. Blue was being about Miltonia. He was meaning just what he was saying. One drink to an old man who ain't never had liquor will get him drunk. So Mr. Broadnax had to be real careful. Just leaving a little town for the first time could be a lot. Broadnax was talking about going on the kind of adventure that could get him killed. But he knew that better than we did. Jim stood up to walk Broadnax to the door. When Mr. Broadnax extended his hand for Jim to shake it, Jim took him in his arms and hugged him.

"Thanks for all that you have done for me. I know it was you who referred me for my first promotion, and I know you always been in my corner. You a good man, Henry Broadnax, but if I ever catch you with your mouth on my dick again, I'm going to smack you into the middle of next week."

Jim was smiling, but he still meant all that he said. "Be honest with yourself. Otherwise, you won't ever know who you are."

Broadnax thanked Jim again. We never saw the man again, but word came from one of his relatives that the very next year Mr. Broadnax had been murdered. When Jim called his family to find out where to send a donation, they were happy to hear from the only man Broadnax had called his true friend. Mr. Broadnax had just settled down into his new life with a man who had lived a life about the same as his. The only difference was that the other man, Tim Greene, had been married for twenty years before he too decided that he been living a lie. He met Mr. Broadnax on his first night in his new life, and they fell for each other. On the day they moved in to their new home, where they planned to quietly live out their retirement years, Mr. Greene's ex-wife killed them both and then killed herself.

Jim sent a donation and a card. On the card he wrote, "It's probably better to leave here being true to yourself than it is to live safely in a lie. Always love Henry's need to be free."

# CHAPTER FOURTEEN

# Casting Pearl Before Swine

*I* done moved through the forest without showing you all the trees. I guess telling you 'bout the end of Mr. Broadnax's life helped me to tell you 'bout what seems like the beginning of ours.

Me and Jim got all kinds of folks coming to the house during the time that we was supposed to have to ourselves. But if I've said it once, you can be sure I'll say it again: You can't enjoy the time to yourself if you don't give yourself to others. We know for sure that Mr. Broadnax ain't tell nobody about what we can do, 'cause he didn't know. Mae ain't say nothing to nobody outside our home 'cause it's only the folks in our house that she done had time for. She ain't even been over to Stan and Irma's farm on account of all the time she sharing with John. So we know when folks say they need our advice and can they come over that Mr. Blue, the man I met over at the market, is acting like the man Jesus heal but tell him not to tell nobody. If you want to keep Blue quiet, you tell him to tell everybody he see, then he won't, 'cause he'll be thinking it's something he want to keep to himself.

Well, folks from all over town and a few counties over get to hearing that me and Jim can help folks with they love life. I guess it didn't help matters none when they see Stan and Irma out on what they called dates. Folks said you would swear that they just met and were in their twenties the way they were carrying on. We started with about two or three folks every day or so, then it got up to every two hours. When folks wasn't coming for they own self, they were coming for someone they love.

"Ain't nothing we can do for them," Jim would say, all determined. "Folks got to seek they own advice."

Most times, even though we already knew it, the stand-ins would admit that they were the one with the problem after all. At first, me and Jim would talk to folks together, then it got to be so much that he would talk to the men, and I would talk to the women. No matter how much folks are willing to venture out in they sex life, country folks are too proud to let on that they do. I was glad to see that same school crossing guard that I heard thinking 'bout that little boy on the day I first got the gift of hearing. Jim was about to take him into the kitchen, but I speak to his head and say, "I'll do this one, Jim." Jim look at me kinda funny, and I could see that my mind-blocking was getting better. Jim's brother, John, explained to me that the mind has many compartments, or rooms, like a house. Thoughts come up from the basement and rise to the attic. When me and Jim first started hearing, we were only picking up on what had come up to the attic.

"Learn to go down the stairs, Louella," John say. "Then you can hear it even before the person knows that it's what they're thinking."

Just when you think you done gone deep in life, you find out you still up around the shores. I knew I was way farther along than the folks that was coming to see us, but comparison is really what killed the cat. Looking at what somebody else ain't doing will block the view to where you need to be going. So I started "going down the steps," as John called it, and found that the closer you get to the basement, the worse the smell got. Sad thing is, most folks don't even know what done crawled into the basement and died, or what was left there by their old dead relatives. Some of that stuff don't even get uncovered, and it's just left there for our children to have to deal with.

Well Ron Jones, the school's volunteer crossing guard, seemed to be the kindest man in town. He volunteered to do anything that included children. "I love kids," he always said. And he meant it, but his idea for love ain't have nothing to do with God's idea.

"Good to see you, Louella. I've been told that you and your husband can help folks in the love department."

I saw that he was getting ready to ask me what he needed to do to win the hand of Georgia Grayson. Now, she just happened to be the single mother of that very same boy that I caught him watching, but I was trying to act like all I knew was what he was saying.

"Apparently, she was very hurt by her ex-husband, and she's having a hard time learning to love. Mr. Blue didn't give me any details, but he told me that if anyone had a problem, he knew personally that you two were the ones to help. He had nothing but good things to say about you.

" 'Don't even bother to go to no psychic,' he told me. 'You tell her the problem, and Louella Johnson will help you out.' Everyone at the PTA meeting was whispering about how you've helped Mae. She looks a world better. God knows she was getting harder and harder to look at."

Now, I know that "hate" is a strong word, but it's in the Bible for a reason. Mr. Jones was hitting on the six things that God hates, and on the seventh, which is an abomination. God hates haughty eyes, a lying tongue, hands that shed innocent blood, a heart that devises wicked plans, feet that run rapidly to evil, a false witness who utters lies, and one who spreads strife in the community. I wanted to hit him, but then I got a better look in his basement. All that had happened to him as a child, and to the childhood of the man who did it to him, was stinking like an old corn in a tight boot on a hot day. The bodies of his molester and the ones before them were piling up in that basement 'cause they had never been caught, but they were trapped there just the same. That's the thing about misery and suffering. If you clean it up, it can pass itself off like a way of life, when in fact it's just a way of death. But when I use to watch TV with Lucy and Mae, one day I saw what I use to think of as pure evil folks on the Phil Donahue show. It was a group of men who call themselves "men who loved boys." Now, they was all suited up and called theyselves "professional" people. Most of them were hidden behind a screen, but they was talking 'bout how they ain't have nothing to be shame of. "Why they hiding then?" I ask for my own hearing. That's when Mae say that the world don't like what they don't understand. Then she tell me that I'm too country to get it. I was wondering how if I'm so country, why she was eating my food and watching my TV? I ain't say nothing more back then, but a whole lot done happened since. I know now that folks is hiding 'cause something in their life done taught them the purpose of shame. It come to let you know that you into stuff you ain't got no business doing, or that you should be doing it at home with another adult who's willing and able with the blinds down. Before you go judging me on account of me and Jim ain't always been behind a pulled-down shade, let me just say, we learning to. Besides, we got too busy the other night to get to the business of the shade.

Anyway, Mr. Jones was going on and on about what he could do for Georgia Grayson and her two young children.

"She needs a good man in her house, and everyone knows how much I love children."

Anybody up on the roof would have no idea what was in the man's basement. It's hard sometime to watch folks do wrong even when you know the wrong that's been done to them. Still, if you can see a person's path, you can understand how they got to where they are. I look at Mr. Jones dead in the face.

"What's the real reason you want to marry this woman?" I ask him.

I was giving him what my children called "the eye." It must have been passed down to me from my mother. She surely got it from hers. I don't even know when I'm doing it. I can just tell from my kids' faces that I must have a look that means business. Mr. Jones kept on going with the story he was trying hard to believe.

"I know that a single mother has a hard time when she's trying to raise her children alone. I would love to help her and her children."

This time he was talking real slow, like I musta been slow or something myself. Now, if you taking notes, write this down. When a person tell you their love for you is all about fixing you up and what they need to do for you, run in the other direction and run as fast as you can. Love is not on one side or the other. It ain't all about what I can do for you. Love is about what we can do for each other, and what each other can do for the kingdom of God. Most folks recite what they call the Lord's prayer without ever believing that it can be done. I really want to see God's will on earth just like it is in heaven. When folks come together in true love, they can play they part in making it so, 'cause God *is* love. Love ain't about lust or stuff or looking like you somebody. It sure nuff ain't about finding somebody to fix you or getting somebody you can fix. Love is about God's will on earth as it is in heaven.

Well, I give Mr. Jones a chance to tell himself the truth so I ask him one more time, "Why you really want to marry this woman?"

He got so slow in his talking that this time I thought that one of them bodies in his basement was working him in slow motion.

"I believe that she needs a man like me."

Well, that did it. Righteous indignation set in, and I opened my mouth before thinking, which I know ain't got nothing to do with righteousness. But falling down don't make you bad. It's staying there that 'cause you to lose the race. I done told you that it was my talking that got us into a mess of trouble. Well, I'm about to tell you what the talking was. I tell Mr. Jones that he know that that woman ain't really what he trying to marry, that it's her son, and if he ever want to set his life right and end that circle that somebody else got him caught in, well, he needs to start by being true to his own self. I do believe that had it not been for Jim rushing into the room, Mr. Jones would have hauled off and coldcocked me.

"Louella Johnson, I don't know what kind of operation you running here, but I do indeed intend to sue you for slander."

"I wouldn't do no suing or nothing else you thinking 'bout," Jim say.

"Where do you people get off accusing me of, of . . ."

Mr. Jones couldn't even finish saying what he knew he was. Now, you know by now that my house ain't that big. All the folks who were coming over to see us would wait they turn in the living room and on the porch 'cause it was still real nice out, and me and Jim would talk to them either in the kitchen or over in the dining room. I was in the dining room with Mr. Jones when he started throwing his cover-up fit. That's what I call it, but Mae say it's "playing the nigger." She apologized for using the word again, but said that she thought that for him it fit. Mae say that playing the n-word is trying to act madder than the other person ought to be on account of something you did. They try to be madder than you will so you won't get mad at all. Mae know this 'cause she done had to deal with all kind of men, and since most of them were cheaters, they were mean too. You can't try to sneak around and not get mad about it, 'cause a cheat ain't nothing but a child in an adult's body still trying to get everything they want just 'cause they think they should have it.

Mr. Jones was screaming and hollering like we was doing something to him. Now, Mae had learned from John why we were able to do some of the things we were doing out. She never even questioned it. Coming up in the church and ending up in all the pain she had seen had taught Mae enough about the dark side of life to know that the bright side had to exist. When you been in darkness for a real long time, it only take a little candle to shine like the day. Well, our kindness to Mae had been all the lamp she needed to believe that what we had was coming from God. It didn't hurt none for her to have the love and attention of one of the most wonderful men I have met next to his brother, my husband, Jim. Now, I know we ain't ever gonna be perfect, but we s'posed to strive for it anyway. It's funny how folks can live halfway and then give up. Like how they get married and respect all them things the preacher say in front of God and everybody else, but in the back of they heads they thinking, "Well, if it don't work, we can get a divorce." I ain't coming down on divorce. God always provide a way out of something that truly ain't supposed to be. But folks use divorce like people do vitamins, they take them after they get sick and expect it to make everything better.

Well, Mr. Jones got to hollering like he crazy. "How dare you suggest that my intentions toward Mrs. Grayson are anything but noble?" He came tearing through to our living room like some kind of crazy man, which he had to be with all the mess he had in his basement. Folks who were already embarrassed to be there started getting purses and husbands and trying to get gone. You can't speak correction to a fool, 'cause you gonna end up getting correction for yourself. We let Mr. Jones go and all who were leaving with him.

It didn't take no time at all for folks to start getting word about me and Jim running some kind of sex advice psychic something or other. I sure wish truth could travel as fast as a lie, 'cause if it did, we'd have a much better world to live in. After that, people did continue coming to our little house. Most of them were just coming to see what we had going on. The rest were wanting what we couldn't deliver, some special love potion to trap somebody who didn't want to be trapped or to control somebody who wanted to be free. If they stayed around long enough to get the truth, they got it, but it really wasn't what they wanted to hear. I had a much greater understanding of what God meant about casting pearls before swine. When folks don't know that they got a good thing, they gonna treat it like it's trash. One piece of gold in a pile of mess don't make it into a pile of gold.

CHAPTER FIFTEEN

# Loving the One You With

*D*espite the Mr. Jones mess, all kinds of folks start to come over. Some with broken hearts, some who needed to mend hearts they done broke, and some who ain't never know love. These were the hardest for me. It was like trying to teach somebody how to swim when they was 'fraid of the water.

One day Miss Fontain came by. She work over at the little public library. I call it "little" on account of it's in a small house. But she got it crammed full of books that can take you all over the world. That woman love knowledge and information, but when it came to putting it to use, that's another story. Now, I'm about to go off on one of my thoughts, as my son call them. But I got to say this. I have never been one to collect things that don't work. I admire folks who can have all them pretty little knickknacks and things. They dust them and take care of them like they a child or something. I ain't one for all of that. If it don't do nothing, it can't stay in here. Oh, I love nice pictures and things. My daughter, Lena, can sure draw, and Jim made a frame for each and every one of her pictures. We got them up everywhere 'cause they do something. They add to the room in a way as to remind you there's more to the world than what's in a house. Them pictures help me think outside of where I am, and some of them tell stories of who we are as a people. When it comes to coins or stamps or thimbles from other places, I just can't get into it. Plus, I can't be dusting and looking at all that just to see if it's still there. What I'm trying to say is this: Collecting things just for you don't really make your life bigger. Now Miss Fontain had collected up a whole mess of books and information, but she wasn't big on sharing it or putting it to use. I'm trying to be nice, but I just need to go on and say it. Miss Fontain was mean. Seem like if she knew as much as she had learned, she'd have been nicer. She didn't 'low no whispering in what she called *her* library. She surely didn't want no laughing. Kids were never let in there without an adult, which if you ask me, and I know you didn't, is a sin and a shame. Some kids ain't got no adult that cares if they read or don't. Reading can take you away from your troubles and some kids got more troubles than the law allows. Not letting them come in to get away from all that gonna keep them locked in trouble.

I ain't know a lot about Miss Fontain, except that she came here right out of school from up North somewhere. Seem to me that she would have gone to a bigger city where she could find a nice young man to love. I use to think she love books more than she love people. Well, I said "use to," didn't I? Fine, then you know that I'm 'bout to get to the point.

Miss Fontain came over one evening after she figured most folks had already gone home. Now, I'ma be true with you 'cause that's how I try to live. I never saw that young woman real good. She's 'bout average height, average size, with an average face. Beyond that, I ain't see much more. When she come into my house, I could see her better. It's all in how we think about people. If you only see them in a library, we only think of them around books. Take Deacon Smith. He's a church deacon and a school janitor. If I didn't see him all in his black suit on Sunday all fine like that, I would not know he's the same man in them green overalls and taking up garbage during the week. Miss Fontain was like that away from books. She seem less average somehow, more at peace with herself, which gave her some glow. It was funny in a way to me, 'cause you would think that a person is more beautiful when they in they element. I guess, for Miss Fontain, it was the opposite.

Miss Fontain, bless her soul, had a reason to be mean. She ain't never had the loving of a man, or woman for that matter. She sat down and poured out her heart like a farmer pours out feed. She did it in handfuls. Look like just when you thought she was through, she had another heap to scatter. It was a slow start, but when she get to going, she was really going.

"Mrs. Louella," she say, "I don't know why I'm here, but I knew I needed to be."

I ask her how she hear about us and just what it is that she think we can do.

"Everybody's talking about you and Mr. Johnson, Mrs. Louella," she say. "They say you got the gift of heart-fixing."

Well, I'd never given a name to what we had come up on, but I guess that was as good a name as any. Jim say that a few would come by expecting us to have some kind of medicine that would get them up and keep them there. Well, they problems weren't like the ones me and Jim start this whole thing with. Those men had to deal with not being able to do the do 'cause they done did what they did all over the place and with too many strange women. I hope you know what I mean, 'cause being able to hear make me really not want to talk bad on womenfolks. God knows they got a mess of problems, and now I see that they got generations of stuff piled up. Jim tell them men that if they fix they heart, they fix their stuff. A few left mad, but one of them, Mr. Thomas, from over in Stansville, say he know just what Jim saying and he gonna get right on it. He say he been cheating on his wife and then treating her like she was the one catting around. Mr. Thomas say a prayer that day and ask God to forgive him and make him strong enough to do what's right. He ask Jim if he should confess to his wife all that he had been doing. Jim told him she probably already suspect something, 'cause women are like that.

"You don't need to tell her everything. Why keep stirring in a pot that's already done? Just let her know that she was right in her thinking." Jim say to him. "And tell her you want to set things straight. Pray with her like you did with me, and you'll get to the truth of what's ailing you. Cheating ain't usually about how good somebody else look to you. It's about how bad you think you look to yourself."

Mr. Thomas called back a few days later to say thank you and so did his wife. She sews real good and told Jim if I ever need anything at all, to please let her know. That's why Jim think that "heart-fixing" is a good name for what we do. We try to help folks see what we can see and hear about they heart.

Well, Miss Fontain told me that she overheard two

women talking about how one of them had been here and how we helped her get over some man who was driving her crazy. I remember the woman too. Now, don't go thinking I got something against big people when I tell you this, 'cause I've already pointed out, I ain't hardly no stick. In any case, Nellie James' daughter, Mara, has been a big girl from the day she was born. She came here the size of a one-year-old child. Like to bust her mother in two. Well, the child screamed and hollered a whole lot, and Nellie had to feed her first to get any peace. Giving somebody something to keep them quiet about something else don't ever solve no problems. You just make them hungry for what you giving them all the time. Plus, you training them on how to get it. Mara knew how to get food. She'd just throw a fit. Well, as you have by now guessed, she got bigger and bigger to where she is today. She's a real big girl, and she's a pretty one. Now, there's lots of men who like them real big like that, which is good 'cause there is always somebody for everybody. But there is also folks who will use what they see as your weakness to get all they can from you.

Mara met a man like that. After he told her how pretty she was and how much she made him feel lucky, he convince her to give him every penny she earned and whatever she could get from her mama. Then after she felt all that he was telling her, he commence to calling her every fat, ugly name he could find. Now I don't care where you go, you can always find dirt. But when you find it, you ain't got to live in it. What I'm saying is there will always be men and women like the one Mara found, but she did not have to choose to make her bed there. Even after the man threw her out of her own apartment and took up with a couple of other women, that young girl kept on telling him she loved him and would do whatever he wanted. Her mama got to thinking that the boy had worked some kind of roots on her.

Whenever folks get to talking like that, I tell them "Greater is he that is within the godly, than he that is in the world." If you get low enough, anybody can step on you. Trick is to not lower yourself. Well, Mara was doing just that. And that boy didn't have to work hard at making her feel no lower. Her mama sent her to me on account of Mr. Blue told her to. Ole Mr. Blue was still in folks' business, but now he was in there to help. I have always believed that if you ain't using your talent for good, it will be used for bad.

Well, Mara came here begging me to help her get her man back. She say she know he love her, but some woman done gone and took him.

"Can't nobody take from you what was truly yours," I told her.

Now, I could already see the real reason her mama sent her. Her mama want her to let that no-good fool go. But I ain't let her know that I know.

"The way out is back through," I told her. "What he do for you that make you feel he love you?" I ask her.

She was about to tell me the stuff that happened when they first met.

"This last week," I added.

Well, she get to stammering and picking at her long, fake nails that somebody told her look good. She had on a real long hairpiece too and a lot of shiny necklaces and stuff. When my kids were small, they loved to play dress-up, but they hated to take a bath. I got to thinking on that, and it came to me that Mara was the same way. If she spent some time walking and reading, she'd look and think a lot more of herself. Well, that's not what she was there for, and I knew that lesson was down the road a bit.

"Well, I haven't seen him much this week," she say into her chest.

"Okay then," I say. "What about this month? What has he done?"

Now, if I didn't know how bad she was hurting, I'da tried to sing that Janet Jackson song I heard one of my grandkids singing. *"What have you been doing for me lately?"* I think that's how it goes. But, just 'cause I thought it don't mean I had to say it. When she couldn't think of nothing, I asked her what that was telling her. Do you know what that chile had the nerve to say? She say he been busy on account of that other woman, and if she would leave him alone, he would be able to love her again.

I look at her hard and say, "Mara, are you sure?"

She thought for a second and answered just that quick. "Yes, I'm certain of it."

When she said it, her voice went all up high like she ain't as sure as she saying.

"If your love was that strong," I ask, "how could anybody come in between unless he want them to?"

She look kinda hurt when I say that, and I let her sit in the hurt that she had help to make long enough to think about getting out.

"Mara, why do you love this man?" I ask her, knowing that this gonna cause her to start getting true.

When John ain't out on them long walk-talks he have with Mae, he teaches me all kinds of ways to use this gift. Because of that, I can see what's going on before Mara do. It start slow. She got to breathing real hard and heavy, then she got to sweating. All a sudden she burst into tears. When I say burst, I really do mean it. That girl raise up off my dining chair and get to swinging her arms and panting like them wild animals on the *Animal Planet* do when somebody trying to put them in a cage. Jim came rushing toward the door, but I threw him the thought to slow down. He came in slowly and put his arms 'round Mara, and he rocked her real slow. I stood back 'cause I knew my part was done. Mara's ranting turned to sad weeping. "He, he" was all she could manage for a long time. Then it came.

"He the only man ever tell me that I'm pretty and that he love me."

Jim kept on rocking her for a good while. And then Jim tell her that love ain't never been no reason to act crazy.

She start to come to herself and said, "I want him for mine."

There it was. She was doing what she always did when she wanted something: screaming, hollering, and acting out 'til she got it. Saying it out loud helped her to see it for herself. Mara really broke down then, and when she did, Jim told her what she needed to do.

"Leave that man alone, and tend to yourself. Mara's got a lot of fixing that needs to be done," he say. "When you love you, you can see real love coming." Jim ask her if she gave that man money, even though he knew the answer.

"Yes," she say. "A lot of it."

"Well, you give most folks lots of money, and they will do and say whatever you want. But money only work for a while, 'cause nobody like to feel like they being bought."

Mara cried some more, and Jim let her. Then he told her to take some time to see who she was.

"You go over to Stan and Irma's farm. Tell them I sent

you there. They need some help with they crop, and you can stand the time with the earth and your own thinking."

I wanted to laugh 'cause I knew Mae was supposed to be there working, but I guess it would be good for anybody in Mara's condition to work off her worry.

"Yes, sir," Mara tell Jim.

"You take some time from your job and go on and stay there for a week. Then we'll see what we see."

Well, Mara did just that and some. From what Miss Fontain overheard, and I already knew, Mara quit her job at the grocery store and started working over at Mr. Stan's, keeping books and helping to organize the workers they had, mostly folks that was heading over there 'cause we was sending them. There was even a man over there that had an eye on Mara, but she told him she needed more time liking herself before she let somebody else like her.

# CHAPTER SIXTEEN

## Books of Life

*M*iss Fontain was hoping that I could do for her like I had Mara.

"What do you want help with?" I asked her like I ain't know already.

She put her head down and left it there for a long time. You could tell that she was not used to asking for help.

"I want to be loved." She said it like she was demanding something of me when she caught my eye. "I need to be loved." She said it softer and with the pain that she was feeling.

"What is love for you, Miss Fontain?"

I could tell that she wasn't expecting something that

smart from my Southern, country self. I'm not big on borrowing books, and I don't lend them. If I want one, I go over to House of Knowledge in Savannah and buy what I want and whatever else the owner Glenda and Alvester tell me that I need. I usually get more than one copy, 'cause one of my kids or somebody gonna want to read it. When they ask to borrow mine, I give them the second copy. But I know 'cause Miss Fontain ain't seen me in her library, she thinking that I don't read much. If she had gone up to my bedroom and my daughter Otha's room, which now looks like a library, she sure would be surprised.

"Love is what I don't have," she say real sad.

I give her a minute to feel what she telling me, then I say, "You don't have a lot of other things, but they ain't love. I need you to tell me what you think it is, Miss Fontain."

She sighed real deep, and I could see her pushing her way through to get to what she was trying to say.

"Love is having somebody to care for me and me for them. It's coming home and knowing that somebody is there or going to be. Mrs. Louella," she saying, finally looking up, "I want somebody to make love to me like they do in some of the books I've read. I want them to want me so bad that they feel like they burning."

Miss Fontain was going on so 'til I thought she might be burning.

"You ain't never made love, have you?" I ask, using the words she use.

She shook her head no and turned her face to the wall. No wonder the woman was so hard on folks. She had to be way in her thirties.

"Why you wait so long?" I ask her.

"My mama," she say.

That's when it came to me that I was back to listening in the upstairs. I had not gone down to the basement to see the things that had really caused her sadness.

"My mama used to touch me down there," she said. "Then she beat me and called me such dirty names 'til I thought I was dirty. I used books to escape her presence, but she was always there waiting for me. Even after she died, she found a way to torment me in my sleep. Sometimes, when I'm awake, trying to do normal things, I hear her voice. If I look at a man, and he looks at me in that way, I hear her tell me that I'm a no-good, dirty whore and that I need to be beaten. Mrs. Louella, she was so mean. I've read enough on it to know that the cycle didn't start with my mother. I suppose the same thing was done to her."

"You're a bright, beautiful young woman. You deserve love," I tell her. "But you also deserve to know all that love is."

She looked at me kind of curious.

"It's some of what you said, but it's more than that too.

You surrounded by love every day. When you helping somebody read something to escape the pain they in, that's love. When a child comes into that library and checks out they first book, that's love. When an old person from 'round here that ain't done nothing but hard, physical labor gets to sit down and read a book that you picked for the library, that's love. Now, truth is harder, but what's harder still is hearing the truth that you been missing."

Miss Fontain had told me some terrible things about her life, and the whole while, she ain't shed one tear. Now, when she hearing about the love that's been right in front of her, but she couldn't see, she commence to crying big, old tears. Them tears flowed like a faucet somebody done left on for so long that it can't be shut off too easy. I let her cry 'cause she needed to.

"I have never cared about the folks who come into my, I mean the, library. Most of the time I saw them as some sort of necessary nonsense that I had to put up with in order to collect the books I wanted. I hated that old man and the child checking out their first book. I didn't see them as important or even deserving of such precious gifts. Maybe it was me who was not the deserving one after all."

Miss Fountain said this and got up to leave. I could feel that she took this harder than she had her own life. I could also see that she planned to end that sad life of hers.

"Sit down," I tell her. "We ain't done."

She started to protest, but I wouldn't let her.

"We got work to do, you and me. I sure do need your help. It will give me a chance to get what you need and some of what you want."

Miss Fontain wasn't trying to hear me, so I had to stand up and shake her by the shoulders real hard 'til she came to. When she did, she started to cry again. This time I held her the way her mama should have. I held her and hummed while she cried a good cry, the kind that comes when you tired of living the way you been and you trying to catch enough wind to move forward. When she calmed down, I told her what I needed.

"I bet you done read all the books in the library, huh?"

"And then some," she tell me.

"You think if I give you a certain topic, you be able to match a book with it? Say I write down something 'bout adventure in the future? My grandson likes all kinds of *Star Wars* stuff, but I sure wish they was a Black book like that."

"That's easy," Miss Fontain said between sniffles. "*Wild Seed* by Octavia Butler or *Aftermath* by LeVar Burton."

"Okay, how 'bout if I want a book about family lives?"

"*Long Walk Home*, Connie Briscoe."

"So if I send somebody to you with a subject, you can recommend a good book?"

"Sure," she say, getting ready to ask how it would help her. "But I don't see—"

"You don't have to see," I tell her. "Ain't you ever hear that sometimes love is blind? Now, most folks say that mean that love can't see all the bad in somebody, but it really means that you should have blind faith for love, not the person you trying to love."

"Mrs. Louella, you are much more insightful than I would have ever given you credit for being."

I tell her, "I know, that's my disguise, chile. It keep folks from expecting too much from me so they can get what they need more better."

I winked at Miss Fontain to let her see that even I knew I shouldn't be saying "more better," though I will continue to do so.

"What do I do in the meantime with my emptiness?" she asked.

"You do what I say, and that ain't gonna get a chance to last too long."

I could tell that Miss Fontain was having a hard time believing me, but I also saw that she was having a hard time trying not to.

"Alright, Mrs. Louella."

"Oh, before you go, I need you to find a book on the subject of some kind of cardatutra thinking, something like that," I said, trying hard to act even more country that I already was.

For the first time that evening, Miss Fontain was

smiling. "You mean Kama Sutra. It's the tantric principles of lovemaking."

She was blushing hard, but I didn't wait long enough for the blush to become embarrassment.

"I'll need a book on that. Can you get it for me? I'll send someone over for it."

Well, Miss Fontain got that book alright, and a whole lot more than she bargained for, but I'll tell you all about that when it's time.

# CHAPTER SEVENTEEN

# Reaping What You Sow

*I* done told you how much I love books. Jim say that he sometimes get the feeling that I love books more than I love him. He know better than that. Still, he like to tease me. One of my favorite places in the whole wide world, not that I been to that many, is House of Knowledge over down Savannah way. Alvester and Glenda own it. They the cutest couple of book warriors you'll ever meet. Now, before you get to wondering why I call them that, I call them that on account of folks who deal in books and take they job serious are like Harriet Tubman on that Underground Railroad; they setting minds free. I told Alvester and Glenda that one day, and they just laughed. They heard way over in Savannah what was going on, and they come up to see 'bout it for theyself. Before now, they had never been to me and Jim's home, so we sure were shocked to see them.

"Morning Mr. Jim, Miss Louella," they were saying through the screen door.

"Hey y'all," I yell back.

We been getting all kinda company, but most of them were folks wanting something. I could feel from Alvester and Glenda that they had something to share with us.

"Lord, looky here," Jim said teasing. "My wife done special order so many books that y'all had to bring them up here, ain't she?"

You know that Jim knew better, but he was happy to see happy folks too, and that always got him to teasing.

"We been hearing 'bout y'all all over the place. What you got going up here, y'all?" Alvester asked.

Now ain't nothing cuter than some educated country folks who choose to keep they country ways. They got more education than my son got, but they don't talk or act in none of them siddity ways. They love where they come from and how they is. Alvester met Glenda in college at Howard University up in Washington D.C. Even when they went North, they kept hold to the country. They were both getting the schooling you get after your undergraduate studies, like my boy Neal is doing. One day Alvester heard Glenda talking to some of her friends. Love is a powerful thing. That boy fell in love with her voice before he even laid eyes on her. When he did see her, it sealed the deal. They been together ever since. Before meeting each other, they had plans to be professors and what not, but they came back to Savannah, which is near both they hometowns, so they could be close to family and roots. Then they took it upon themselves to open a bookstore for they community. House of Knowledge has been like a rest stop for many a weary soul.

Alvester and Glenda sat down in our kitchen while I cook up a mess of food that only country folks would eat for breakfast. Mackerel, grits, eggs, and pancakes. I warmed the fried chicken from the night before and pulled out some peach preserves. After we ate and laughed about how me and Jim done got to be the talk of the town, they got to the reason for their trip.

"We brought you something I think you'll need to see," Glenda say.

She opened a large bag and lifted out a book that was wrapped in an old cloth. She did it real slow and gentle like. But I could not read its pages with my thoughts. Jim was having the same problem.

"This is the reason why we do what we do," Glenda say, handing me what I could see was a precious gift.

"It was the first knowledge we came upon," Alvester say.

Then two talked like twins, finishing sentences and ideas for each other and sometimes together. Jim sat next to me in that breakfast nook. We didn't open that cloth right away. Something was telling me to be still, so I was. After a while like that, I open that cloth and see the book that changed us even more than the gift had. It was older than any book I had ever seen. Now, I can only tell what I know to be true. That book was about me and Jim. I get the shivers just talking 'bout it. It didn't have our names or even what we would look like, but it talked about us and folks like us who would be able to help others heal by listening to all that had happened to them and what they needed. Now, me and Jim done seen a lot in these few weeks, but this thing made us weak. We commence to read that book and saw that the gift that we thought we got on account of my Grandma Sadie showing us how to love had been there all along. We had to unlock it by going farther into each other. Now I know why you can't really feel what you want physically if you ain't willing to pay the price spiritually. Folks done gone from one kind of sensation to the next, thinking they got to find a position or a partner that can please them when the pleasure is in the spirituality. I'm too excited telling you this 'cause I'm running in front of myself. I need to read to you some of what me and Jim read to each other, and you'll see what I'm talking 'bout.

CHAPTER EIGHTEEN

# Are You The One?

*L*ife *always has a way of working itself out. I for one am glad of that. My life was not what I wanted for me or my people, but that's ok because all of that's gonna be worked out later on. Now, I'm writing these things down 'cause that's what I'm supposed to do. Everything ain't always about you, but you'll find out later on that they was still for you. I'd tell you my name, but that don't matter none. This ain't about me. It's about whoever read this and puts it into action. I been watching the things that done happen to our life and love for a long time. I've lived for more than one hundred years. I reckon that wasn't for me neither. All things start someplace and work their way back around, so here is the beginning. You see where you fit into the circle so you work yourself into it.*

*My people are perishing. Their life is leaving them, and they spirit along with it. The sad thing is, they don't really see it. Sometimes what feels like freedom can really be slavery. But I'm a keep on watching so others will know and point to the way to life. I have known the power of love, and I've felt the sting of hate. But I'm here to tell you that love always wins. Yes it do.*

*I have seen my brothers used like animals. They move them from one stall to the next, hoping to get my sisters with child just so they can have more hands to do their work and bodies to do what they want. This ain't natural, no way it is. Children come here to show us men how to love, and to be separated like that, well, it tears you down, tears us down as a people.*

*I see the women ashamed of who they is 'cause their child didn't come from love. They love them children just the same, but it something lopsided 'bout that love. Look like they mad at them while they trying to love them at the same time.*

*I see those children trying to live with only the lopsided love of they mother, and no love from a daddy. This ain't right. Love can't grow in a place like this. When the children are sick, everything gonna be sick and die.*

*They grow up trying to find the love they mama and papa didn't have. They know it's not allowed so they try and sneak off, loving behind barns and in places where can't nobody see them. But love ain't s'posed to hide. It needs the daylight and old folks' blessings to shine on it and water it. It need to be nurtured and taught.*

*Years go by, and love been tormented, but it last. 'Cause no matter what else is, love gonna be. You watch what I'm telling you.*

*We s'posed to be free now, but still we ain't living like we was meant to. Folks can't stand us doing for ourself and each other so they burning and tearing down what little we got. They don't want our love to be 'cause that's the real power. Them that know can see that. Many work 'longside us in love and it changes them. That's why we was brought here in the first place, to bring this peace throughout the world. I'm looking close now, 'cause look like to me most of us done forgot that. We ain't telling our stories to our children no more so they can know and tell they children. I'm getting tired, but I know that love gonna win. I'm putting this down. The next one gone come and pick up where I left off. It's up to you to write what you see and to tell others how to live in the love that's been took.*

*Is you the one to do it? To carry this on?*

Jim and I read that and couldn't believe the gift that we been given. We read on and sure enough somebody else came along and continue to write.

*I am the one. My name is not important. This work, the love is important. I found these papers looking for something else. I guess that's the way love is. When your heart is right, it will find you no matter what it is you think you looking for.*

*I better do what I'm supposed to do 'cause this is not about me. It is however for me.*

*I see our lives continue on a path that is not sure. We are not sure of ourselves or of the love placed within us. Many see, more do not. Children are scattered like dandelions in the wind.*

*Who will love them? Who will teach them all that they are? Nightriders come and destroy families. The children watch. They don't know the power of love so they are fueled by hate. The children of nightriders also see and learn. Many are living the hatred, but more are taught to fear. This fear, this need to despise the thing you don't understand is worse than the hatred. Hatred is loud, clear, and can be destroyed by itself. Fear and shame can go on and on and re-create the truth in a way that lets you be as you are—ignorant, fearful, ashamed.*

*Where are we? Many answer the call of love. They raise their children and other children to be bold as lions but meek as lambs. There are those who are born, and some yet to be born, who will walk in the way of love. Still, they will fall down because they have not learned the secret of winning the battle against hate. You cannot love humanity but despise and mistrust your family. The secret lives in ourselves. We have walked in the way of our captors, and I fear that the war will continue beyond my years. I must leave this work. It came to me in my late years. The battle has just begun.*

*Are you the one to read this and pick up the path? Will you watch and tell others? Will you live in the love? Are you the one?*

*It's my time to write, but I don't feel like the others did. This love thing should take action. We need to move now* 'cause the man got his foot on our throat and we can no longer sing the story of slavery. Them old Negro tunes have no place here. This is a battle of wills. We gotta love and build our families back however we can. Women must learn their rightful place in this movement 'cause that's how the man is trying to take us out. He gives our women jobs and leaves us to fend or fight. I'm choosing to fight. Yeah, I'm the one. But it ain't gonna be like the others thought.

I'm picking up these papers because they were mine to pick up after all. My husband, man, my brother is dead, not physically, but spiritually. He hated the oppressor so much that he learned to be like him. Children understand this. Hatred is the opposite of love. But in order to hate something, you must have love for it, that kind of love that adores but does not work. If you want power, you must take it from your oppressor. If you want peace, you must walk in love. When you have peace, you have power. I know the secret of winning this battle. It is simple and seems insignificant. We must love our children, love your husband, your wife. Do not stray. Stay with the love you have chosen and learn the joy of satisfaction. I must go on, but others will come. Are you the one?

Me and Jim kept on turning the pages. The more we read, the more we saw into the basement of our people.

We have picked up the work, and we do what we can to watch and to pray. The patterns seen by the first continue.

This time, however, no one has forced us to do this, the greatest blow to all of humanity has been to destroy the truth. Men make children from one stall to the next. These children grow up without the love of that man. The men move through life without learning the power of loving through the eyes of their children. Women have become strong, resilient, unbreakable. In many respects this is good, for who will care for the children if they are too weak to do so? But their hearts have hardened to the peace that surpasses understanding. They go from one man to the next looking for the love that they didn't find in the last. Hardened by the cycle of their life, they turn away from their mothers' love, who in the their later years find the true meaning of this life. Unable to connect, these women, mothers and daughters and sisters, are not able to pass what they have learned to one another.

Passion rules the day, and love must be held at bay. Even the sweetness of our passion is kept a secret because we have now learned shame and hatred over humanity and peace. We can no longer merely watch and record. The chosen ones must stand up and be counted. We must be the light for others to see. We must stand in the gaps. It's time to speak truth to power, to walk in love boldly. Fear no one. Tell of the peace that comes in knowing who we are and whose we are.

Love your children. They don't have to come from you to belong to you.

Love your parents. They have hurt in ways that you won't because they loved you.

Love your mate. Spend as much time and energy keeping them as you did trying to get them.

Love yourself and your community, your people. They are one in the same.

Above all, love God, your creator, your maker. Love God more than you love this world and the things of this world. They will not last. But love never fails.

When you get love, are walking in love, have learned to be loved, teach it to others. The time is now.

Are you the one, the chosen? Will you walk with us? Will you stand in the power of love?

# CHAPTER NINETEEN

# A Life of Learning

Jim and I wept for as long as we read. We knew without a doubt that it was us that the book was talking about. Jim's voice was pounding in my brain.

"It's us, Louella. That's what this thing is been about all along. It's us."

All of a sudden, we could hear Alvester and Glenda talking to us. "We gotta go now," Glenda said. "We probably won't be seeing you no more. We moving on. Our job down here is done."

Jim and I were a bit confused. Then things seem clear as the new morning.

"Alright," I say out loud, 'cause I'm still set in some of my ways.

In my mind I could see them going from town to town setting up bookstores, showing love to children, old folks, and young ones. They told of the love we needed to have for one another and showed others how to heal. I was glad for them to have this gift so young, but sad for all the work they had to do.

"Don't worry 'bout us, Miss Louella. We gonna have y'all praying for us and lifting us up. We'll be fine."

"Gone girl," I said, fighting back my tears. "Get out of here 'fore I don't let you leave."

"Come on, Glenda." Alvester was laughing now. "You know Miss Louella will do it too."

Jim laughed with him, and then he did something I've never seen him do with our children. But just 'cause I ain't seen it don't mean it didn't happen before. With the palm of his hand, he touched Alvester's head. He touched his heart, then he grabbed his hands and pulled him to his chest and hugged him. They held each other like that for a while. When they were through, both of them were crying. Now, I know that something passed between them, but I don't know what it was. I reckon I wasn't s'posed to. That was fine with me, 'cause I done seen and learned a whole lot in the past month, more than most folks find out in they whole lifetime.

# CHAPTER TWENTY

# The Storm Before the Calm

Me and Jim didn't say nothing for a few hours. But we was thinking plenty. We got to thinking on all the ways we could use our gift to show others how to love more deeply and be connected to all that they are.

Have you ever been happy and sad at the same time? Well, if you ain't, just keep living. We felt kinda funny 'bout who we were in the scheme of things, if you know what I mean. That's when we saw it, the reason for our sadness. Now, sometimes things can slip right by you without you noticing. But other times, it's like you watching in slow motion, and you can't do a thing about it. That's what this was like. We saw him coming the same time we felt it. With all the wit and wisdom we got, that was too late. Mr. Jones, the volunteer school crossing guard, came through our door with a loud crash. I found out later that the crash was the sound of Jim's brother falling on top of him. It's a good thing somebody was paying attention. He was on the floor with John on top of him when we came to our senses and ran in there. Mr. Jones was struggling to get to the gun he came in with when Jim came down on his hand with his size-fourteen shoes. That man let out a scream that could've raised Lazarus again. I got the gun and put it in the pocket of my housedress. Now, 'fore you get to thinking I'm some kind of fool, I ought to tell you that I took the bullets out. Well, John had picked Mr. Jones up from the floor like you would a baby who done crawled too far.

"Talk," he say up in the man's face. "Talk now."

Mr. Jones commence to saying how I done ruined his reputation all over town, how I been telling folks that he's a child molester and that everybody ought to stay away from him. He said that he intended to do away with us one way or another, and that if it wasn't him that there would be folks who'd do it for him.

"I got friends in high places. I am not alone, you know. You think you know me, Louella Johnson. You don't know the half. There's more like me in this town and the next than there is like you. We take care of each other."

Now, part of me knew that Mr. Jones was for a fact

crazy, but the other part knew that what he was saying was true. It scared me a little, then I remembered that the battle was a spiritual battle, and that it was already won. We just had to see it through. I walked up to him like I had just been told to do. I was walking in love boldly. John let him loose so Mr. Jones would know that I wasn't afraid.

"Man, what you say is true, but that don't make it the truth. Everything that you done did to a child shall be visited on you and those like you. There was a window of time for you to get things right, Mr. Jones. But you chose to hold to your ways, so now that window is shut. I want you to listen to me and listen good," I said.

Now, y'all remember earlier when I told you that my talking got me into trouble, but it was my talking that got us out. Well, this was the time it got us out.

"You are right. There are more of you than there is of us. And if you know all that, Mr. Jones, then you also know that greater is God in us than the one that's within you. You are the filth that you do. It didn't have to be that way. I know that the things you did were done to you, but I also see that you done chose to be what you is. You scheme and plan to destroy young lives just to get what you want for yourself. The fact is that you been at it for years. What's worse is that you plan to be at it for many more and that you ain't just been hurting the kids. You got some in training to be like you. You, Mr. Jones, gonna die in your own mess. There was a time that I could've—no, would've—helped you. You missed your opportunity when you came in here like a fool trying to hurt me and mine."

I moved up closer to Mr. Jones' face so he could see the strength in my heart that was coming through my eyes.

"You go and tell them so-called friends of yours, if they ever lay a hand on any more children, they gone have something to deal with."

Now, you must believe me when I say that if anybody had seen this, they'da laughed just like Mr. Jones tried to. Like I said before, we ain't old, but we ain't young neither. I'm standing here promising this man what we would do like I was in a karate movie or something.

Well, like I said, Mr. Jones was about to laugh, then he got the picture that we all sent to his head. He saw and probably tasted the curse that he had put on himself. I was just the one to speak it. The things he had done were visited on him. Not the same things, but the vile way he made the children feel. Well, Mr. Jones left our house crying out in the pain that he was just beginning to feel. Later on that day, the sheriff found him in front of the school, crying for help. They took him to the state hospital, where he later died. Folks who worked there said he kept yelling, "I see it. I see it. Please make it stop."

Well, our Mr. Jones ain't all that there is. I know that. But I also know that you reap what it is that you sow. I said that we had been feeling sad and glad at the same time. Alright, I'm getting to it. I really don't like it when folks got something to tell you, and they talk all around it 'fore they get to it, just like I'm doing now. Don't worry, I'm getting there. Sometimes the ride is better than the trip itself. Well, John and Mae had gone and got married. John had been blocking my thinking so good that I hadn't seen the things that led up to this. They had been walking and fishing and laughing and loving. I told you earlier that their loving wasn't physical, and it wasn't. Yes, there was a lot of hand-holding and hugging, but Mae had had more of the physical than me and Jim have had in all our twenty-some years, including the past few weeks. She was in need of good, old-fashioned love. What she needed was someone to see all that she was and to acknowledge it while she could do the same. Well, Mae was beaming like the morning sun.

"Come over here, girl, so I can hug you," I tell her after I had seen the truth.

She cried, and you know I did right 'long with her.

"Louella, I have lived like a fool. It took me all these years to find myself and to find love. Believe me, I tried."

"I know," I tell her. "But love ain't in most of the places we look."

She smiled and let me know that she knew just what I

was saying. Ain't it funny how time will let you say something one day but won't another? My daddy used to say timing is everything. Right then and there, I got a glimpse of what he was saying. I'd explain it to you, but now ain't the time.

Mae had another surprise for me. She took me up to Neal's old room and showed me the other thing I hadn't been seeing. Turns out, Mae had a talent after all. Any mother who says they know their children completely can't be telling the truth. You just ask the parents of those kids over in Colorado. You know the mess I'm talking about. Them kids who built a bomb right in their parents' garage without nobody knowing 'bout it. I ain't saying that anything like that could go on in this house, but stuff happens without us knowing. Which is why no child of mine had what today's children call privacy. Anyway, John had blocked this from our view 'cause they wanted to surprise us. My son Naim, as I now call him, 'cause he say it's his new name and I got to respect it— well anyway, Naim had been teaching Mae how to paint. Turned out that she was better than he was, way better. Mae had a true gift. She could paint the things we need to see when we trying to get back through all the pain of our families and they families. In them paintings was the hurt and the history of who she was. Folks always pray to get out of something, when they should really be praying to for the right tools to drill through it. When you go through it, you get the lessons you need.

I walked in that room, and there was art everywhere. Bright paintings that were too painful to look at, but too beautiful not to. Oh, I wish I could tell you all of what I'm trying to say. One painting was of a little boy. His eyes were big and sad, but there was still a bit of hope in them. When you first looked at it, seemed like his mouth was turned down, then you could see that one corner was turned up kind of smiling like. Seemed like he was saying I'm down, but not for long. There was a painting of a girl in a dirty dress. She was on a long, dirt road. In the background was a house, and on the steps stood a woman with her hand on her hip. She looked mean. You could tell that she had been yelling at the child, but the child was in another world. It was a happy world where the little girl planned to stay. All of Mae's paintings felt like a whole story. Well, this was another one of them few times that I couldn't say nothing.

Jim was all beside himself. He was wiping tears back and hugging Mae, then hugging Naim, who had joined us.

"Boy, you crazy as a bug, but you sure are beautiful to me," Jim say.

Naim knew that was a big compliment, and he took it that way.

"Well, now, what you think?" Mae ask me.

I gave myself a second to think before I say anything.

"Mae," I said real slow. "I think you found your love."

We smiled and cried for all that was and would be. I knew right then that she and John had planned to leave this little country town. And I know that I wouldn't see my friend no more. Mae had found a healing love, but she was still dying. Before you get religious on me, let me tell you this. God can and does heal, but healing ain't just for the body. Sometimes it's restoration of the heart so you can go on to the next place. God had answered my prayers. Mae was healed for the life she had chosen, the life that was destroying her true self.

Mae and John had a whole year together. They spent it loving life and one another. Now that may seem kinda sad at first, but think about it. A whole year of love is more than most folks get throughout they life. They spend more of it fussing and trying not to care than they do appreciating everything around them. That's how Mae lived out her time. John went shortly after her 'cause he had lived ten lifetimes in one, and he was tired. He told me a lot before he left though. Most of it came in a letter he sent out to me just before he and Mae made their transitions.

*My Dearest Louella,*

*Thank you for the joy you have shown me. Mae and I grow more and more in love with each and every breath that we take. I have known many things, but I have never held the heart of one so true, so pure. I know what God felt for David, the man after his own heart. While David did many things that were not pleasing in the eyes of God, his heart had such good intentions. My Mae's heart has only sought after love. Because of you, she can now see her entire life more clearly.*

*There are many things I did not share with you, Louella. There are even more that I cannot. Suffice it to say, God knows. Some things will be necessary on this journey; I will let you know now.*

*Louella, what you and Jim have come into is something that has been in our family for many generations. It has not always manifested itself because of the time or the conditions within which we have been living. We are watchers. Those whose job it is to study the mysteries of life. I know that before now, life for you seemed simple, but life is anything but. There is more going on right in front of us that we can see, or better yet, care to. Mysteries unfold by the minute through a story or in something a child says. The clues to these mysteries are in the sky and in our hearts.*

*You, Louella, have been chosen to listen and to tell others. My brother, Jim, is a fortunate man. He was blessed to have chosen properly in his youth. While the gift has been in our family for generations, it sometimes manifests itself through the one we have chosen to unite* with. Louella, you are the one. Jim is gifted because of his connection to you. We knew this would happen many years ago. Jim was never told any of this, so as not to influence his will. All he was told was that there was a brother who would make things clear. I was that brother. He knew of me but had never ever seen a picture of me. I was sent up north when I still a child. Louella, understand what I am telling you. My family protected me from a road that was prophesied when I was still a baby. My father was told that there were two paths before me, one of destruction and one of wandering. The wandering road would take me away, and my mother and father would never see me again. But it would lead me back to my brother and you. On the other road, he saw me staying with my family, growing up with Jim and loving him, but despising him at the same time. There would be a competition between us for everything, including your heart. I would win, but destroy you after I did. My mother begged my uncle to find a way to change that course. She did not want to lose any of her children. My uncle told her that things were as they were. She cried for days and would not eat or drink. At the end of this period, she said that she had come to understand. She had seen a vision of the two roads of life. One road was the will of God, while the other was an attempt at undoing it. At anytime in life, she said, we are on one or the other. If we do not do God's will, we will seek to tear it

204

down for everyone else. She sent me away with an uncle who raised me. When I was old enough and had begun to manifest my gifts, he told me my truth. I wanted to come back into the arms of the mother I saw in my spirit. She was crying for me and praying for me daily. By then, I knew enough to know that I could not come back yet.

I've lived all over the world, waiting for the sign that told me my time had come. That's when I met Naim. You have raised beautiful children, Louella. Do not worry about the path they appear to have taken. They belong to you. You and Jim have placed within them and around them real love. They will walk that path. Remember Abraham took Sarah in the twilight of his years.

Louella, the book that was given to you holds the key to winning this battle. Nothing happens by chance. There is a plan, but there are always roads. Continue to stand for love in the ways that you are learning. Teach others the power of forgiveness and the strength that comes from humility. Love every moment of every day. We don't have time for anything else. There is a way that seem right to man, but that way is death. Show them the right way, Louella. These things I'm telling you may seem like a tremendous burden. I must tell you that they are. But on the other hand, the road to destruction is no less tiresome. And as my brother says, if you're going to be tired doing something, make it the right something.

Again, my sister, I thank you for all that you are

*and all that you do. Continue to walk the path of peace
and love. We will see you on the other side.*

*Your brother-in-love,*
*John Johnson*


Well, wasn't nothing I could do but cry and thank
God. So I did. The whole time I was reading, I blocked
my thoughts for Jim so he couldn't read me reading that
letter. When he came home from work that day, I met
him at the door. I was smiling and so was he.

Good loving is like hot buttered biscuits. If you want
them to be good, you gotta put a lotta work in them. The
more you roll that dough, the fluffier them biscuits
gonna be. If they get just the right amount of what's
needed, they gonna rise and rise. When they come out
the oven, you just can't wait to taste them.

By the time we got in the house, he was already reaching up my dress.

"Jim Johnson, you could at least wash your hands
first," I say, playing.

"That's what I'm trying to do now," he whispered in
my ear. "Come here woman so I can bathe myself in you."

# Epilogue

"Everything works for those who love God
and are called according to his purpose"

$\mathcal{N}$ow 'fore you go thinking I left ends loose and my hem is falling, let me tell you some of what happened and is still happening in our little town.

Miss Brown from across the street took up with Mr. Wilson. That caused as much of a scandal as Mae did coming to church. But those two up and left here 'cause Mr. Wilson said he too old to be talked about. They down in Florida watching sunsets and taking cruises every month just so they can enter the newlyweds' contests on them boats. Turned out that Mr. Wilson had more money than anybody 'round here, and Miss Brown had more sense than most. She was so lonely 'cause she had not been loved. She was crazy 'cause that's what pain will do. But now she doing fine with Mr. Wilson. They send us a picture every month from the SS something or other.

Remember Miss Fontain, the librarian? Well, she got the more-than-she-bargained-for that I told you about. I told her that I was gonna send somebody over to pick up that Kama Sutra book. Well, I did. I sent my son Naim. Long story short. Wasn't nothing in that book them two didn't try. When they got tired of all that crazy, curious stuff, they came down to earth. Funny thing was, they thought nobody knew. Now you know when a woman gets something she ain't ever been getting, it shows. Miss Fontain started telling folks to call her Sheila, a name nobody had ever heard. She got to dressing in bright colors and even started wearing her hair like Naim's, which is in them dread things. Now, it ain't take no gift for folks to see whose hand was in her cookie jar. By then, we had so many scandals, as folks were calling them, that Naim and Sheila didn't matter that much. Most folks were happy to see her happy though. I got to sending people to her to get books so they could keep learning whatever it was they needed to learn. I would write a few words on a piece of paper and give it to them to take to Miss Fontain, as I still call her. They'd go over there and hand her that slip which might say "work problems," and she'd turn around and get *This Just In* by Yolanda Joe. Then folks would read it and come thanking her like she had the gift too. In more ways than one, she did. I've learned to turn the light of my gift on to someone else. I don't need no more attention on me and Jim than is already there. We know that others are watching us, waiting for a chance to take us out. But love never fails. It wins all the time. Yes, it do. Yes, it do.

## *Acknowledgments*

*I*t all started when Blanche Richardson at Marcus Books in Oakland and San Francisco asked me to write a piece for a collection of black erotica. I laughed and said, "You gotta be doing something to write something." Then Blanche laughed and said, "Use your imagination girl." I decided to do just that. That's when I got a visit from Louella Johnson. She got to talking and I couldn't get her to stop. Now if you knew me real well, you'd know that I am not the one to get all personal out in public. So the fact that Louella stopped by to see me was a big surprise. I will always be grateful to Blanche for enabling me to invite Jim and Louella into my head and my heart.

In previous books, I have thanked many of my friends

and family members for their support of my life and work. I don't want to do too much of that in this book out of fear that folks will accuse me of getting tips from them.

There are those I do need to thank. I am forever grateful to my agent and sister-friend Victoria Sanders who believes in my work and my madness, thanks for always being there. My editor, sister, and mean jewelry maker, Janet Hill, may you find the love of your life (she's a vice president brothers). My management team Direct Touch, thanks for praying, laughing, and working with me, you have been true friends. My family that seems to keep growing, you are the love that I need.

I have also decided to acknowledge the artists whose music and works have inspired me. Thanks: Maxwell, Bethany Pickens, Will Downing, Nancy Wilson, Keith Jarrett, Coltrane, Buckshot LeFonque, Kadir Nelson, Juliet Segneious, D'Angelo, Baaba Maal, Maggie Brown, Donnie McClurkin, Me'shell Ndegéocello, Mint Condition, Donny Hathaway, India Irie, Patsy Cline, Gil Scott--Heron, Marc Anthony, Kymani, Nina Simone, Patti Labelle, Vinx, Jubilant Sykes, Wynton Marsalis, Kathleen Battle, K.D. Lang, Jessye Norman, Carl Thomas, Freckle, Tim Cunningham, Lenny Underwood, The Brothers at Ironwood, The Praise and Worship Team of Inner-City Faith Fellowship, Phyllis Hyman, Phoebe Snow, Roberta Flack, Aretha Franklin, Amon Rashidi, The Roots, Mos Def, Maxwell, (did I already say Maxwell) and Maxwell, and the brother from Amistad, Djimon Honsou. (I know that he is not an artist, but he sure is a work of art).

For Ishmael and Mary Johnson, married sixty-six years. And to all those who know what it means to have an everlasting love.

Special thanks to the couples who keep on keepin' on and show us how to love; folks like Tina and Spencer (Lover) Bernal, married forty odd years, Lloyd and Carmen Cooper, thirty-two years, Susan Taylor and Khephra Burns, Ruby Dee and Ossie Davis, Harold and Gloria Thompson.

By the by, In every one of my books, I like to highlight a bookstore that I find special. House of Knowledge is a real bookstore in Texarkana, Texas. Go by, call or email Glenda and Alvester, they are as country as they are powerful.

## ABOUT THE AUTHOR

*Bertice Berry, Ph.D.*, is an inspirational speaker, sociologist, and former stand-up comedian. She is the author of four works of nonfiction and the novels *Redemption Song* and *The Haunting of Hip Hop*. She lives in Solana Beach, California.